CW00523812

DISCARDED
SHROPSHIRE LIBRARIES

SURGEON ON SKORA

Theatre Nurse Judith Henty and surgeon Brad
Hamilton make a splendid surgical team. What does
it matter that outside the operating theatre they
simply can't get on?

SURGEON ON SKORA

BY

LYNNE COLLINS

MILLS & BOON LIMITED
London · Sydney · Toronto

*The text of this publication or any part thereof may
not be reproduced or transmitted in any form or by any
means, electronic or mechanical, including photo-
copying, recording, storage in an information retrieval
system, or otherwise, without the written permission
of the publisher.*

First published 1984

© Lynne Collins 1984
Australian copyright 1984

ISBN 0 263 10473 7

SHROPSHIRE COUNTY LIBRARY

64 / 4 / 88

Set in 10 on 12 pt Linotron Times
15/0484–52,339

*Photoset by Rowland Phototypesetting Ltd
Bury St Edmunds, Suffolk
Made and printed in Great Britain by
Richard Clay (The Chaucer Press) Ltd
Bungay, Suffolk*

CHAPTER ONE

LONG fair hair whipped by a blustery wind about her face, hampered by a heavy case and a shoulder bag and weary from a long day's travel, Judith walked along the stone sea-wall towards the ferry that would take her across the stretch of grey, choppy sea on the final part of her journey.

Nearing journey's end, the thought of new surroundings and strange faces and the many miles from everything she knew almost made her turn back to the train that would soon be snaking along the coastal railway line towards the dear and the familiar that already seemed so remote. The plaintive cry of seagulls as they twisted and turned and swooped across the grey sky seemed to sound a lament for the past while the steady thrum of the small boat's engines seemed to echo the apprehension she felt for the future.

A fine rain was falling and the distant cluster of islands was almost obscured by mist. One of them, Skora, was Judith's destination. Largest of that particular group of the Western Hebrides, it boasted a town and a few villages, a number of farms, and a handful of factories that provided employment for the islanders.

Recently, an American company had opened a factory for the production of soft drinks on the outskirts of the town of Skyllyn and Judith was on her way to work for the Jefferson Corporation in the clinic that it had established for its employees and also for fee-paying patients.

It had seemed an exciting adventure when she first applied for the job. Now, Judith wondered if she had done the right thing to come so far from home and family and all her friends at Hartlake, her training hospital. Skora seemed a million miles from anywhere to someone who was used to the bright lights and sophistication of London. She comforted herself with the thought that if she didn't like the work or the place or the people she needn't stay a day longer than the six months stipulated in her contract of employment.

The bundle of magazines that she had thrust beneath her arm slipped and fell to the ground and would have been whipped away by a spiteful breeze if a tall man striding in her wake hadn't bent to scoop them up and return them to her.

Judith's swift smile and murmur of thanks were met with a dour, unsmiling nod that left her feeling rebuffed and wondering if all the Western Islanders were so unfriendly.

The ferry-boat as well as its crew looked elderly and weatherbeaten and Judith hesitated at the foot of the gangway while the rest of the passengers streamed on board. She put down her heavy case and brushed the long strands of hair from her face and regarded the only available means of transport to Skora that night with a doubtful expression.

She was jostled by a boatman who carried the last of a pile of boxes and crates that were being ferried across to the island that evening. She moved hastily out of the way and he glanced at her curiously.

'Bound for Skora, lassie?'

She smiled, nodded. 'Yes.'

'Best get on board. We're off away within minutes.'

'How long does the crossing take?'

'Time-table says forty minutes but the sea's against us.' He shrugged. 'Could be as much as an hour.'

Judith visibly wilted. An hour! It would be nearly dark by the time she got to Skora and she then had to make her way to the Jefferson Clinic. Miss Macintosh, the clinic administrator, had told her that a car would meet her at Skyllyn where the boat docked. If it didn't, she would probably fall by the wayside and never be seen again, she thought wearily, longing for a meal, a hot bath and a comfortable bed.

She humped her case up the gangway and crossed the deck to the passenger cabin. There were few people travelling and no sign of the tall man who had rescued her magazines although she had watched him board the boat only minutes before herself.

Taking a seat, she tried to whip up her flagging enthusiasm for the venture. Only another hour and she would be on the lovely Isle of Skora, about to begin an interesting new job and meet some interesting new people, she told herself brightly. She had been due for a change after five years at Hartlake and Miss Macintosh had painted a glowing picture of the clinic with its up-to-date equipment and highly-qualified staff. Judith had been thrilled to get the job and all her friends had been envious. Life on an island sounded so romantic and exciting.

It was only because she was tired and rather dispirited by the unwelcoming weather that it suddenly seemed a narrow and limiting way of life, with escape to the mainland apparently dependent for much of the time on the battered old ferry-boat and the vagaries of the sea.

The heavy smell of diesel oil was in her nostrils and the throb of the engines reverberated through her slight frame. Judith tried not to feel slightly sick, reminding herself that she was a good sailor and trying to ignore the swell of the sea as the boat rocked, straining at its moorings in the freshening wind.

Within minutes, just as the boatman had warned, there was the unmistakable sounds and bustle of imminent departure and the last-moment arrival of another passenger who bounded up the gangway, exchanging friendly greetings with the boatmen. Tall and broad and red-haired, bright blue eyes rested with interest on Judith's slender figure in jeans and Aran sweater.

Their eyes met and he grinned, engagingly, Judith looked away. Tired, hungry and apprehensive, she was in no mood for a shipboard romance, she thought dryly. He was young, good-looking and obviously friendly and she wondered if he was a native of Skora or a recent import. Or just a holidaymaker.

Despite the fine rain and a chill breeze, she went out on deck to look wistfully at the receding mainland as the boat ploughed through the waves towards the mist-shrouded islands.

It was early summer but she had been advised to bring warm clothes and now she was glad of the thick sweater she had pulled on over her shirt before stepping out of the train into the pure but cold Highland air. She leaned against the deck-rail, watching the seagulls and the foaming wake of the boat and the dwindling buildings and diminishing harbour of the Scottish fishing town. Then she turned to look at the islands on the horizon.

Perhaps it was the vast greyness of sea and sky and the

unsmiling face of the distant Skora that depressed her. But there was a heaviness about her heart as though she was heading for disaster—and she felt sudden panic at the thought of making her home in this alien part of the world among strangers. She felt quite sick with dismay and apprehension at the thought of the next six months on the unknown Skora. Or was it just the revolt of her stomach after the poor, hurried meals of the past two days and the lurch of the boat as it struggled with the mounting wind and waves?

Judith became aware of the man who stood further along the deck, the tall man from that earlier brief encounter. He was studying her rather than the sea and the sky and the island that was obviously his destination, she realised.

He seemed oblivious to the rain and the chill although he wore only a thin jacket over an open-necked shirt and light-weight slacks. Judith saw him brace his broad shoulders against the buffeting wind and admired the bronzed column of his throat, the lean but powerful build, the proud set of his dark head and the masculine good looks. Even from a distance, she sensed the potency of his physical magnetism.

Their eyes met and a strange *frisson* of an awareness that was both unexpected and unwelcome rippled down Judith's spine. He nodded, neither friendly nor unfriendly, merely casual recognition. She smiled slightly, not too sure, not encouraging.

She wondered if there was a shortage of women on Skora. For both this dark stranger and the red-headed young man with the confident grin seemed to regard her with interest, she thought wryly, thankful that five years at Hartlake had taught her how to cope with male admiration and attentions. Amorous male patients were an occupational hazard for any nurse, of course. In a teaching hospital, so were medical students and young doctors and Judith had learned to recognise the different types very early in her training.

The light-hearted, fun-loving flirt who worked his way through each new set of student nurses and was too obvious to be dangerous, for instance. The too-serious, heavy-going bore who only wanted a girl to be a good listener while he propounded theories and detailed his ambitious plans for the future that didn't include marriage for a good many years. The unexciting, undemanding and rather unreliable sport who liked to have a girl-friend in tow but really preferred the company of his fellow-students, the rugger matches, the rags, the drinking sessions. The solitary who had no time or inclination for anything but medicine, often haunting the wards and getting under the feet of the nurses long after rounds were finished and often attractive enough without knowing it to have all the juniors sighing over him.

Happily, there were always a few of the pleasant and dependable kind who could be relied on for liking and friendship and escort on social occasions and didn't expect too much in return. It was among those that Judith had found her boy-friends during her years at Hartlake when she was too involved with nursing to want a serious or lasting relationship with any man.

At twenty-three, she was still a virgin—and not just because she had never been in love. She was mature enough to know that loving and sexual experience didn't always go together. She had never been sufficiently tempted to go to bed with any man and therefore had always found it easy to say no or to avoid the kind of situation where consent might have been taken for granted. She valued her virginity and she didn't intend to part with it lightly.

Now, the dark, glowing eyes of a stranger looked into her own for a long moment. Judith felt her pulse quicken for absolutely no reason but a strange kind of apprehension that was almost excitement. He was much too attractive in a too-physical way, she decided—and no doubt he knew it!

She turned slightly away from him and kept her gaze fixed on the Isle of Skora, becoming more discernible with its blue hills and craggy coastline as the mainland was left further behind them. She ought to return to the cabin where it was dry and warm if stuffy but she was reluctant to have a stranger suppose that his interest had driven her from the fresh air that was keeping sickness at bay.

'You're looking green, lassie,' declared a warm and very pleasant voice. Judith turned swiftly to find friendly concern in a pair of bright blue eyes and a smile hovering about the lips of the tall young man with the burnished red hair. 'It's a rough sea the night,' he went on, producing a small hip flask from the deep pocket of his anorak. 'Take a wee dram.'

Judith smiled, slightly wary. She shook her head. 'Thanks—but no thanks,' she said firmly.

'It will help the sickness. It's brandy.' His smile deepened to warm the good-looking, rather youthful face. 'You needn't fear me, lassie. I'm a doctor.' It was matter-of-fact, reassuring.

'A doctor!' Judith quickened with new and very natural interest. 'Then we're in the same line of business. I'm a nurse,' she told him, promptly forgetting the vague queasiness of her stomach in the relief of finding a friend. He was young and pleasant with a disarming smile—*and* he was a doctor.

'Student?'

'SRN,' she amended, '*and* midwife.' Having worked hard for her badge and the extra qualification, she was proud of both.

He was surprised and it showed. Her slight build, the flyaway fair hair and the general appearance of carefree youth had deceived him, he realised. He had taken her for a teenager but she was obviously older than she seemed. He sought and found the signs of responsible maturity in the very pretty face with its faint dusting of freckles, a slightly stubborn chin, steady grey eyes and sweet mouth. 'Here on holiday?' he asked lightly.

She shook her head. 'Starting a new job.'

He looked at her with sudden interest. 'Would you be the nurse from London that Ailsa Macintosh at the Jefferson Clinic is expecting the day?'

Judith smiled, unconscious of the impact of the golden smile that had cheered patients and enchanted young doctors throughout her years at Hartlake. 'I think I must be,' she agreed. She held out her hand impulsively. 'Judith Henty . . .'

'Jamie Sinclair.' Clasping the slender hand, he smiled down at her with a gleam of admiration and rather more than friendly interest in the bright blue eyes.

'Do you work for the Clinic?' she asked eagerly.

'No. I'm in general practice in Skyllyn, actually. I know most of the staff at Jefferson, of course. We send in the occasional patient. Ailsa's a good friend. You'll like her,' he promised.

'I'm sure I will.' Judith withdrew the hand that he seemed reluctant to release. 'I'm getting cold,' she said lightly. 'Why don't we go inside and talk? If you could tell me something about Skora and the clinic and the people then I wouldn't feel quite such a new girl when I get there!'

As they walked towards the cabin, he put a hand to her elbow to steady her against the rocking motion of the boat. Judith smiled up at him, willing to go more than halfway towards liking him if only because she was among strangers in a strange place. She was used to making up her mind quickly about people and trusting to her judgment. She decided that Jamie Sinclair was reliable. He was good-looking and pleasant and friendly and she felt that knowing him might be an asset in the coming months.

A strand of her long hair was whipped across her face by a sudden gust. Turning her head, putting up a hand to brush the hair out of her eyes, she met the scrutiny of a pair of dark eyes. She had quite forgotten the tall man who still leaned against the rail, too distant to have heard their conversation over the sound of sea and wind but near enough to have realised the rapid falling into friendship of two strangers. There was a gleam of irony in his eyes as he looked after them and a sardonic smile was hovering about a sensual pair of lips.

For no reason at all, she experienced a shaft of dislike . . .

Plying the good-looking Jamie Sinclair with eager questions and being reassured by the answers as well as his good-natured friendliness, Judith scarcely noticed the rest of the journey and suddenly they were docking in Skyllyn's pretty harbour. It was almost dark and the small town that clustered at the foot of the hills was a fairyland of twinkling lights.

She had expected her arrival on the legendary Isle of Skora to be momentous, memorable. Somehow, it passed in a flurry of shouts from the ferrymen, the clinking of chains as the boat was secured and the gangway lowered, the thud of boxes and crates being unloaded and the bustle of disembarking.

The tall stranger had stayed on deck throughout the crossing, a remote and mysterious figure defying the elements. Now, he was first to leave the ferry. Watching him make his way down the gangway and along the stone jetty with brisk and purposeful stride, there was something so distinctive about him that Judith almost turned to ask Jamie who and what he was – and then dismissed him as the doctor took her arm to escort her to dry land, carrying her case.

'How do you propose to get to the Jefferson Clinic?' he asked with the light, friendly concern that was so acceptable to someone who was very far from home. He smiled down at her, reassuring. 'It's a few miles out on the Skelbeg road and you'll not get a bus at this hour, I'm afraid. But my car is at your service. Just say the word.'

'I'm being met,' she assured him with rather more confidence than she actually felt. 'But thanks, anyway . . .' She paused by the ferry gate and held out her hand. 'You've been such a help and I'm grateful.'

There was smiling warmth in the blue eyes. 'You won't forget that we have a date?'

Judith smiled and shook her head. He had promised to show her something of the island. 'My first free day,' she agreed. 'I'm looking forward to it . . .' So she was. He was nice, very easy to get on with, and she might be very glad of his friendship and his company on occasions in the days to come.

When he had vanished into the night, she felt oddly bereft as she stood with her case at her feet, waiting to be claimed. Like a parcel, she thought dryly. She looked round for someone who might look as if they'd come to meet an unknown nurse. There was no one about and no car in the near vicinity. All the ferry passengers had dwindled away except for the tall, dark man who was just emerging from a telephone booth. Judith carefully didn't look at him as he glanced in her direction.

Deep-set dark eyes narrowed as he gazed at the rather forlorn figure in jeans and thick sweater, standing beneath the illuminated ferry sign and obviously waiting to be met. She looked very young and rather lost and he was surprised that such a pretty girl had been abruptly abandoned by an opportunist like Sinclair.

He hesitated, frowning, as a sudden thought struck him. Then he began to walk towards her with sure stride.

Judith stiffened slightly at his approach, remembering the way he had watched her earlier that evening and the look in those dark eyes when she left the deck with Jamie after a very brief exchange. Suspecting that he had quite the wrong idea about her, she prepared to rebuff an overture in no uncertain terms.

'Miss Henty?' he demanded, without ceremony, slightly brusque.

Her eyes widened in mingled surprise and relief. 'Oh—*yes*! I'm Judith Henty!'

'You aren't at all what I expected.'

His glance raked her from head to toe. The words were abrupt, almost accusing, and Judith's chin went up swiftly. 'I'm sorry about that,' she said, tart.

He brushed aside the spark of indignation with a hint of impatience in his dark eyes. 'I met your train at Fergin and ignored you because you looked far too young to be a qualified nurse.'

'I'm twenty-three!' She wondered why his manner should put her instantly on the defensive. It wasn't exactly aggressive, just brusque, very impersonal.

'Well, you don't look it in that get-up,' he told her bluntly. Reaching for her case, he took her by the arm in a firm grip. 'My name's Hamilton. I had to be in Fergin today and Ailsa Macintosh asked me to look out for you. I've just telephoned to tell her that you appear to have missed the train.'

Compelled to walk by the side of a too-forceful stranger, Judith looked up at him with a militant sparkle in her grey eyes. 'Do you make a habit of leaping to wrong conclusions?' she asked sweetly, bridling at that blatant disapproval of her appearance and still smarting from the way he had looked at her and Jamie on the boat as though he thought she'd been an easy pick-up for a man she didn't know.

'Not as a rule,' he drawled, indifferent to irony. 'I don't have to tell you that doctors are trained to weigh all the evidence before pronouncing a verdict.'

'You're a doctor?' Judith's tone was doubtful. He was so high-handed and so brusque and so impersonal that she shuddered to think what his bedside manner must be like!

He escorted her across the road to his parked car before he made any answer. Then he said levelly: 'I'm the resident surgeon at Jefferson. We'll be working together as I understand that you're an experienced theatre nurse.'

'That *will* be nice for me,' Judith murmured.

Producing keys from his pocket, he unlocked the car doors. 'I doubt it. According to your unlamented predecessor, I'm demanding and bloody-minded and a devil to work with,' he said coolly. He looked down at her, unsmiling, dark eyes glinting in the expressionless face beneath the light of a street lamp. 'Which means that I don't tolerate laziness or inefficiency. I believe that you're Hartlake-trained. That's something to your credit, I suppose.'

'Kind of you to say so!' Judith snapped, bristling with indignation. Head high, she got into the car, hoping he wasn't representative of the rest of the staff at the Jefferson Clinic. She wanted to enjoy her brief stay on Skora! Now she wished that she'd taken up Jamie's offer of a lift to the clinic and left this man to look in vain for the nurse he'd promised to meet. Detestable man! Arrogant pig!

Having stowed her case in the boot, Brad swung himself behind the wheel with a glance at the stormy face of the new theatre nurse. Touchy little madam, he thought indifferently. Well, he didn't mean to charm her out of her sulks. He had no time for girls like this one, too ready to flirt with anything in trousers and much too confident of the impact of that pretty face and golden smile on every man she met. Trust Jamie Sinclair to be panting after her before she'd even set foot on Skora! He was a womaniser of the worst kind without heart or conscience who traded on his looks and charm and easy manners.

She would soon learn that the man wasn't to be trusted. He didn't mean to warn her. She wouldn't listen, anyway, he suspected, noting the stubborn set of her chin and the militancy of those lovely eyes. What woman ever listened to good advice once she'd set her heart on something?

'You're a very trusting young woman, Miss Henty,' he commented, without approval.

Judith had been watching the quayside cottages slide past the window as the car gained speed, taking the coast road that presumably led to Skelbeg. She turned her head to look at him, wary. 'What does that mean?'

'It means that you should have asked for some proof that I *am* Brad Hamilton.'

'Oh . . . !' Judith was disconcerted. Then she rallied. 'You knew my name and that I was expecting to be met by someone from the Jefferson Clinic.'

'I might have overheard you handing out that information to Sinclair,' he said dryly. 'I don't doubt that you told him all about yourself. That young man has a very persuasive way with him.'

'Then you know Dr Sinclair . . .' It was impulsive, born of surprise. It seemed odd that professional colleagues should have ignored each other so pointedly on the ferry. They obviously weren't on friendly terms. Judith could believe that a man like Brad Hamilton had very few friends!

'Aye, I know him.' It was curt, disparaging.

Without good reason, Judith felt compelled to defend her ready response to the red-haired doctor's friendly overtures. 'He was . . . kind,' she said, chin tilting. 'I wasn't feeling too well and he came to see if there was anything he could do.'

The surgeon slanted an eyebrow. 'You don't have to explain yourself to me, Miss Henty. I'm not sitting in judgment. I merely pointed out that it can be dangerous for a young lassie to be too trusting.'

It was so avuncular, so patronising, that Judith bridled. 'And you don't have to worry about me, Mr Hamilton!' she snapped. 'I may look like a schoolgirl but I'm quite able to take care of myself!'

'I'm very glad to hear it,' he said, indifferent.

CHAPTER TWO

GLOWERING, Judith lapsed into silence. Disliking him intensely, she sat stiffly by his side as the car consumed the few miles between Skyllyn and the small village of Skelbeg. The road was just a winding, unlit ribbon and it was too dark to see much of her new surroundings. To the right, the sea was a swathe of black velvet below them. Occasionally, they passed a cluster of crofter's cottages or an isolated farmhouse. It was still raining and the wind swept straight in from the sea on a mournful howl.

Judith's heart failed her slightly as she realised that the future was going to be very different to anything she had known in the past. She had left a large teaching hospital for a small private clinic. She had left streets swarming with people and traffic and lined with shops for the lonely terrain of a Hebridean island. She had left friends who provided liking and affection and companionship to work with dour and unfriendly Scots like the surgeon by her side.

She hoped she hadn't made a mistake by coming to work on Skora. It might not be so bad if she didn't have to see too much of Brad Hamilton. He might be disconcertingly attractive with those dark good looks, but she didn't like him at all. Not liking him, it was rather disturbing that she should be so aware of his physical magnetism, his masculinity, the potent sensuality of the man as she sat beside him in the sleekly expensive

Mercedes. It was an unconscious emanation, she knew. Judith tried not to remember the shiver of excitement that had rippled down her spine when their eyes met on board the ferry. It was absurd that she should feel so oddly threatened by a stranger who was too attractive for his own or any woman's good. Perhaps it was just as well that she didn't like him and wouldn't have the least difficulty in keeping him at a safe distance.

'I've been hearing much about you from Ailsa Macintosh,' he said abruptly.

'Really? She didn't tell me a thing about you,' Judith returned sweetly. 'I expect she didn't want to put me off coming to Skora. I gather it's hard to get staff and even harder to keep them at the Clinic. I can see why!'

Something flickered in the dark eyes. She wasn't sure if it was amusement or exasperation. She settled for the latter. Judith didn't think he had a sense of humour, judging by that unsmiling mouth and those enigmatic eyes.

'You don't have to like me, Miss Henty,' he drawled. 'Just do your job to my satisfaction and I'll not complain.'

She bridled at the arrogant tone, very sure that liking was the last thing she could ever feel for this man. 'I shouldn't think that you're easy to please!'

'I'm not. So you'll have to work at it, won't you?' If she wanted to turn a slight clash of temperaments into a full-scale war, so be it, Brad thought dryly. It wasn't part of his job to placate yet another nurse who discovered that living and working on a lonely island in the Hebrides had unexpected drawbacks. Including himself. He knew he wasn't the easiest of men. He was demanding, perfectionist. He didn't suffer fools gladly—and said so. He was quick-tempered and he had a caustic tongue and he'd been known to reduce an incompetent nurse to tears with a few, well-chosen words.

If this spirited young woman was as capable and as experienced in theatre work as Ailsa declared, then it didn't much matter that she'd apparently made up her mind to dislike him. In truth, he'd prefer it that way. He was rather thankful that she seemed to be immune to the good looks that were the bane of his life. He'd suffered too much from women who fell for his physical attractions as though they outweighed every other quality. It was scarcely surprising that he was very near to settling for the level-headed and often critical affection of a woman he'd known for years and could trust not to overwhelm him with emotion or make demands that he just couldn't meet or get in the way of his dedication to surgery . . .

Judith was tempted to tell him to go to hell. The words trembled on her lips but she thought better of it. If she really had to work with this man on a regular basis then it wasn't wise to quarrel with him even before she reached the Jefferson Clinic. It might not be necessary for them to like each other but there ought to be some kind of rapport between a surgeon and his theatre nurse, if only for the sake of the patients. Open warfare over the operating table wasn't conducive to good surgery!

She suddenly realised that the car had turned through an arched gateway and was proceeding along a tree-lined drive to a rambling mansion of grey limestone, elegant with its colonnaded porch and tall, narrow windows and gabled roof. Its eighteenth-century beauty was floodlit to heighten its charm and impressive magnificence against the background of a thickly wooded hill.

Judith caught her breath in surprised appreciation and admiration. 'Is this the Clinic?' She had expected a newly-built and very modern edifice. This lovely house was a delight.

'It is. It used to be the laird's house with a history going back to the thirteenth century. Now, the laird lives on the mainland and his heritage has been sacrificed to line the pockets of Americans.'

The words were harsh and touched with some bitterness. Judith wondered why it affected him so deeply. But she certainly couldn't ask him. He was cold and arrogant and hostile. Not in the least like the warm-hearted and good-natured Jamie Sinclair.

'You don't seem to have any liking for Americans. I wonder why you work for them,' she said, not even trying to hide the instinctive dislike and antagonism and resentment she felt towards him.

Brad brought the car to an abrupt halt in a parking bay. 'They pay well,' he said dismissively. He had no intention of explaining himself to a sharp-tongued Sassenach, he thought grimly.

Judith hoped he wasn't the type who was more interested in his bank balance than the welfare of his patients. She wished she felt more optimistic about working with him. She felt that he lacked the essential warmth and sensitivity of a good surgeon.

At Hartlake, she had been used to working with some of the finest surgeons in the world and she would obviously be critical of the technique and performance of lesser men. But the skill and dexterity of a surgeon's hands wasn't all that mattered. He needed to care, too. Judith didn't think that Brad Hamilton was the kind to care for anyone but himself.

Looking at the lovely old house that had been turned into the Jefferson Clinic, she felt that odd little tingle of apprehension once more. Perhaps it was just the newness of everything that was affecting her so strongly. She had always found it easy to fit into new surroundings and to make new friends. But there was something forbidding about Skora—or was it just the surgeon's cold and unwelcoming hostility towards a newcomer that seemed to chill her heart and fill her mind with foreboding for the future?

Brad glanced at the slight girl with the fair hair cascading down her back, so youthfully pretty, so independent, so sure of herself and so unsuited to life on Skora with its ageless simplicity and unhurried pace. She might be older than she looked and she might have all the right qualifications for the job. But he didn't believe that she would be any good as his theatre nurse. That stubborn chin and the challenge in those grey eyes and the impulsive tongue told him that there would be many clashes between himself and Judith Henty in the coming days. She was the last thing he needed to have around in his life.

'You'll not be happy here,' he said abruptly, very brusque. 'You have to be born to the islands to like the life. A girl like yourself will miss the shops and the cinemas and the discos, the bustle of the city. I doubt that you'll settle.'

'Perhaps I shouldn't bother to unpack,' Judith said tartly, resenting the implication that she had already been weighed and found wanting by an arrogant Scotsman. He knew nothing about her! How dared he assume in that high-handed way that she would hanker for the bright lights? It wasn't the lack of amenities that was likely to drive her from Skora but the hostile natives, she thought angrily.

She got out of the car, head high, wondering why he seemed so set on putting her off the place and the job. Didn't he fancy working with her any more than she fancied working with him? Had he disliked her almost on sight—or did he merely resent her as a newcomer to his precious island?

She had heard tales of the fiercely proud and independent Highlanders with their ingrained resistance to change, their dour suspicion of strangers. The surgeon was obviously bitter and resentful that this lovely old house in its romantic setting no longer belonged to the laird, descendant of the chieftain who had once ruled over the clan who settled on Skora. No doubt he had been born and bred and lived most of his life on the island and disliked the many changes that the years had brought. But that was no good reason for so much hostility towards herself she thought indignantly.

Ailsa Macintosh was a relief after the thinly-veiled antagonism of Brad Hamilton's attitude. Plump and jolly and warm with smiling welcome, she made Judith feel instantly at ease—and she liked the unconventional scold that the surgeon received for failing to recognise the new nurse at Fergin and allowing her to make her own way across to Skora after the long journey from London.

'What a welcome for the poor lassie after coming so far!' she declared in lilting Highland accents that delighted Judith's appreciative ear. 'And you with a pair of good eyes and a tongue in your head, Doctor! Were there so many lassies burdened with luggage and bound for Skora the day?' She shook her head at him in amused reproach.

'Mr Hamilton was expecting someone older,' Judith intervened smoothly. 'Apparently, he didn't think I looked the part.'

There was a slight edge to her tone that wasn't lost on the shrewd Scotswoman. Brad Hamilton making himself unpleasant again, she thought ruefully, wondering what devil it was that got into the man at times. He could be such a charmer when he chose! What on earth had he found to dislike in this pretty girl? Surely she was more to the man's taste than a beautiful but demanding woman who had him running round in circles to please her. Ailsa had little liking for Dr Susan Craigie for all her cleverness.

'Och, he thought you'd be wearing cap and apron, no doubt,' she declared lightly, smiling. 'But you're a sensible lassie to wear such comfortable clothes for the journey. If I was young enough and slim enough, I'd be wearing the jeans off duty, too!'

Brad turned to the door of the office. 'Having discharged my duty, badly or no, I'm away to my dinner,' he said. 'Does Miss Henty begin her duties with tomorrow's list or must I manage with yet another agency nurse who doesn't wish to learn my ways?'

Ailsa looked doubtful. 'I'd thought to give her a day or two to find her feet . . .'

'I'm quite happy to begin work first thing in the morning,' Judith broke in firmly. 'It's what I'm here for, after all.' She met dark eyes with a hint of sardonic amusement in their depths and felt like throwing something at that handsome dark head. He'd deliberately manipulated matters to suit himself, she realised too late. It was infuriating that he'd summed her up so well! 'If you could just give me an idea of the list, Mr Hamilton . . . ?'

After six months of working in Theatres at Hartlake she was familiar with most procedures, but it would be just her luck to be landed with an unknown and intricate operation on her very first day, she thought dryly. She wasn't prepared to risk it.

'A cholecystectomy and two hernia repairs in the morning. A breast biopsy and a hysterectomy are scheduled for the afternoon. I suppose you're familiar with all those procedures?'

He regarded her, unsmiling. The formality of tone and manner was slightly mocking tit-for-tat for her own, Judith realised, bridling.

'Quite.' She knew that he was throwing her into the deep end and expecting her to drown. It would be a pleasure to disappoint him, she thought proudly. He obviously didn't know much about Hartlake nurses!

'Operating days are Tuesdays and Fridays. We deal with mostly routine cases, you'll find. They are treated with as much respect as if we were dealing with open-heart surgery.' His tone was caustic.

'Naturally.' Her eyes flashed indignation. Did he think it was different at Hartlake?'

'We have an efficient team and excellent theatre facilities. But we have been short of a really good instrument nurse with suitable experience. I gather that you have all the right references,' he said. 'I hope you'll live up to them.'

Ailsa saw the militancy in the girl's grey eyes as the door closed with a snap on the tall figure of the straight-talking surgeon. He didn't try to endear himself, she thought wryly.

The like-it-or-lump-it attitude was born of an unconscious arrogance that was usually outweighed by his equally unconscious charm. But that charm wasn't in evidence this evening for some reason. She'd never known him to be quite so unfriendly towards a newcomer. She wondered what had happened between him and this pretty nurse during the short drive from Skyllyn that one could almost touch the tension in the atmosphere. Was it possible that the sensual Brad Hamilton had made an unwise and unwelcome pass and had his face slapped? It seemed unlikely. But one never knew . . .

He was a man like any other and Judith Henty was very feminine with that floating fair hair and heart-shaped face and slight build and the air of fragility that was probably due to weariness. Ailsa had long since ceased to worry about her own lack of sex appeal. The new theatre nurse had it in good measure and she hoped that Judith Henty knew how to handle the men who would soon be in full pursuit. News travelled fast on Skora . . .

She smiled, reassuring. 'Temperamental—like all the best surgeons!' she declared lightly. 'I'm afraid he had rather a lot to put up with from our last theatre nurse and it still rankles. But you'll soon get to know his ways and I'm sure you'll work together well.'

'Once I've convinced him that I know one end of a scalpel from the other, perhaps,' Judith returned dryly.

'You mustn't mind his abrupt manner, you know. He doesn't mean anything by it.' It was slightly anxious. Ailsa didn't want to lose a nurse with such glowing references almost as soon as she had arrived because she couldn't get on with Brad Hamilton. It wasn't easy to get nursing staff to come to Skora or to stay when they did come. She liked this pretty young nurse with her warm smile and candid eyes and it would be a tremendous relief to have a really efficient and reliable theatre nurse on the staff after managing for the past few weeks with agency nurses from the mainland who had little interest in temporary work.

'I won't mind anything if he's as good at his job as he obviously expects me to be,' Judith said smoothly. 'I can always make allowances for genius!' She smiled, inviting the grey-haired administrator to share the joke.

Ailsa smiled doubtfully. The girl's tongue was as sharp as the surgeon's and she suspected that sparks would fly in Theatres until they learned to accept each other. She suspected that it would be too much to hope for mutual liking after such an unpromising start.

'He was impressed to hear that you trained at Hart-lake,' she said gently, pouring oil on troubled waters. 'It has a grand reputation. We're very lucky to have you on our staff and so I told Mr Hamilton.'

'I think you may have been rather too enthusiastic,' Judith said lightly. 'I'm sure he disliked me before he set eyes on me!'

'I'm sure you're mistaken. He's a very fair-minded man as you'll find when you know him better.' It was brisk. It wasn't really etiquette to discuss one member of the staff with another, Ailsa suddenly realised. 'Now, you'll be ready for a hot meal and a good night's rest, no doubt. I'll take you over to the staff annexe as soon as I've shown you something of the clinic. You'll need to know your way to Theatres, for instance, if you're sure that you'll feel up to going on duty at such short notice?'

If she was dead on her feet in the morning, she would struggle to Theatres rather than give the detestable Brad Hamilton the least cause to think her lazy or unreliable, Judith vowed. But she didn't say so. The kindly Scots-woman was so obviously anxious that she should get on well with the surgeon that she wondered dryly just how many nurses he had driven from Skora with his arro-gance and his antagonism. Well, he wouldn't drive *her* away before she was ready to go!

She was really too tired to appreciate the brief tour of the lovely old house with its careful and clever and no-expense-spared conversion to a thoroughly modern clinic. But she listened carefully as Ailsa Macintosh detailed the current intake of patients and outlined her hours and duties. It seemed that she was expected to do some general nursing as well as take over the responsi-bility for the smooth running of Theatres—and her midwifery would come in useful, too. She was obviously going to earn her exceptionally good salary!

More and more people were turning to private medi-cine and the Jefferson Clinic had already established a reputation for high standards of surgery and nursing care. Many patients came over from the mainland, having heard that the clinic only employed staff with the highest qualifications. Doctors were pleased to recom-mend it to their patients and specialists in various fields were always willing to attend a case, knowing they would be ferried to and from the mainland by the company's own helicopter. Employees of the company were treated with exactly the same care and consideration as fee-paying patients, Ailsa stressed. The Jefferson Corpor-ation cared about its work-force.

Judith was impressed.

Later, she was even more impressed by her new employers when she was ushered by a bustling, fresh-faced housekeeper into a small but self-contained apartment in the modern, two-storied staff annexe in the grounds, discreetly hidden from the main building by a clump of trees. It was comfortable and convenient with a sitting-room and separate bedroom, well-equipped kitchenette and bathroom—and it was rent-free. Having secured the best possible staff for its rather isolated private hospital on Skora, the Jefferson Corporation apparently did all it could to keep it.

The tiny Scotswoman handed her the key. 'Come and go as you please. We don't have a long list of rules and regulations,' she said briskly. 'Consideration for others is all we ask.' She smiled at Judith. 'You've some bonny lassies for neighbours and you'll soon make friends. Now, I hope you'll be comfortable and you must let me know if there's anything you lack.'

'I will, Miss Anderson. Thank you!' The golden smile lit up her small face like a shaft of sunshine.

'Call me Maggie. Everyone else does.' She opened the wardrobe door. 'I've hung up your uniform frocks for you. I'm handy with my needle if they want any minor alterations and I don't mind obliging you.'

'Everyone's very kind on Skora,' Judith said warmly, quite forgetting an unfriendly surgeon who hadn't been kind at all.

'Aye . . . well, you're a long way from home and you're only a wee lassie, after all.' She moved towards the door. 'I'll leave you to your settling in. If you drive at all, you'll be wanting a wee car to get you about, by the way. My brother has a garage in Skyllyn and he'll be pleased to find just the thing for you if you mention my name. The last lassie brought her own car and took it away again. But it was more in the garage than out of it . . .'

Left alone, Judith sank into a chair. She felt better for the splendid supper that had been waiting for her in the staff dining-room and for the warmth of the little house-keeper's kindly welcome. She looked about the cheerful sitting-room with its bright cushions and curtains and the shelves just waiting for her books and ornaments to make her feel entirely at home.

She felt better still for her lovely little flat and the freedom that went with it. It was nice to feel that she was regarded as a responsible adult. Sharing a flat with two friends in the Nurses' Home at Hartlake—known as the Nunnery by the medical students—had been fun but restricting. Even in these permissive times, Home Sister kept a careful and too-motherly eye on her charges, staff nurses as well as the first-years. Judith had no desire to lead a wild and promiscuous life but it would be nice to invite someone like Jamie Sinclair for a meal and a cosy evening without feeling that she was outraging all the conventions.

She was so tired that she had to force herself out of the chair to unpack and put away her clothes. Americans certainly did things in style, she thought admiringly, as she moved about the small flat and arranged the few possessions she had brought with her to give a personal touch to her surroundings.

Very soon, she was soaking in a hot and fragrant bath, easing away the jaded, headachy weariness of the long day and dwelling on the niceness of Jamie Sinclair rather than the nastiness of Brad Hamilton. She hoped to see a lot of Jamie. She knew that she would be seeing far too much of the surgeon.

She washed and dried and brushed her long, spun-gold hair until it was a shining, rippling mass of waves and curls falling about her face. Then, feeling that it was still too early to go tamely to bed although she realised that she had a very demanding day before her, she put on a robe and curled up on the couch to review the day's events.

A ring at her doorbell set her heart skittering in sudden panic that her unexpected caller might be Brad Hamilton. Had she left anything in his car? Had he forgotten to tell her something that she needed to know before she went on duty the following morning? Then, chiding herself for such a foolish fancy, knowing it was the unlikeliest thing in the world that the surgeon should seek her out before circumstances thrust them into each other's company, Judith hurried to the door.

'Hi! I'm Marian Somers, your next-door neighbour.' Tall and slim and dark-haired, very attractive, she sparkled with vitality and vivacity and friendliness. 'I'm just making cocoa, the nurse's life-saver, and wondered if you'd like to join me?' Warm brown eyes smiled at Judith. 'It isn't so very long since I was a new girl and I remember the feeling. A thousand questions and no answers!'

The glossy black hair was cut short in a riot of curls and she wore rather more make-up than Hartlake approved for its nurses. Wearing the lilac uniform frock with the silver badge of a state registered nurse pinned to her breast, she had an air of maturity and sophistication that appealed to Judith. Liking the warm smile and the easy manner and the hint of humour in the friendly invitation, she accepted gratefully.

She wasn't too tired to welcome a new friend and she couldn't shake off the feeling that she would need all she could find on Skora . . .

CHAPTER THREE

JUDITH followed the slender, dark-haired girl into an apartment that was a carbon-copy of her own except that it was much more lived-in. It was unusual for a trained nurse to be quite so untidy, she thought, stepping over discarded shoes and hesitating to move a pile of records from the couch although she had been urged to make herself at home. A handbag occupied one of the armchairs, with most of its contents strewn over the cushion. A stack of newly-laundered underclothes had possession of the other chair.

'Just dump that lot on the floor,' Marian advised cheerfully. 'The place is in a mess. I had some friends in last night and haven't had time to clear away the evidence. The party went on until the early hours. Pity you missed it . . .' She made a half-hearted attempt to tidy up and promptly abandoned the idea. 'I'll go and make the cocoa . . .'

While she was busy in the kitchen, with much clatter of crockery and banging of cupboards, Judith looked about her with smiling indulgence, remembering parties in the past that she had enjoyed with her friends at Hartlake.

Empty glasses and half-finished bottles stood about the room at random. A record player had been left on, its turntable still revolving ceaselessly. More records were scattered on the floor by the window. Books and papers were strewn haphazardly on table and chairs. A man's sweater lay in a crumpled heap in a corner. A bra was draped over a door-handle. The open door of the bedroom revealed that the bed was unmade, its covers trailing across the floor.

Judith would have blushed if anyone had seen her own domain in such condition. But Marian seemed quite indifferent to the importance of first impressions. Liking her, Judith closed her eyes to her new friend's rather doubtful lifestyle. After all, untidiness wasn't a mortal sin. And if she was a caring and conscientious nurse what did it matter if she let her hair down when she was off duty?

Marian brought in the cocoa and some biscuits. She plumped on the couch beside Judith and leaned to switch off a transistor radio that had been playing rather too loudly, tuned in to a station that seemed to specialise in broadcasting the latest in popular music. 'I expect it's much too soon to ask what you think of the place?'

'The Clinic? I haven't seen much of it so far,' Judith agreed. 'Impressive seems to be the right word.' Marian nodded. 'I love my apartment, of course. I didn't expect such luxury.'

'It is nice, isn't it? Compensation for some of the drawbacks of the job. But I won't go into detail about those on your very first day!'

'I think I've already met one of them,' Judith said on an impulse that she immediately regretted as she saw a spark of very human curiosity in Marian's brown eyes.

Being a gregarious girl, Marian welcomed the new arrival for her own sake. But having heard through the grapevine that Judith had arrived in Brad Hamilton's sleek and expensive car, she hadn't been able to resist getting to know her that very evening. Now, interest quickened. 'Can you possibly be referring to our devastating Mr Hamilton?' she drawled, eyes dancing.

'Devastating is the word! He flattened me!' Judith retorted, with feeling. 'Doesn't he like women? Or did I just make the mistake of being born on the wrong side of the border?'

'Oh dear! Did he treat you to the Scot and the Sassenach bit?' Marian sympathised. 'Wearing the kilt, was he?'

Judith laughed. 'No! Does he?'

'Indeed he does! On high days and holidays! You should see him in the kilt—tall and broad and handsome with a fine pair of knees, striding over the hills that he says are soaked with the blood of Hamiltons. He's very proud of being a descendant of the Highland Hamiltons who settled on Skora centuries ago. They were a fighting clan, hot-tempered and always at war with their neighbours, apparently.'

'Certainly a direct descendant,' Judith murmured, very dry.

'His uncle is the laird. Brad can't forgive him for selling Hamilton House. Not just to Sassenachs—but to American Sassenachs! He hates the whole set-up.'

Judith stared. 'But he works here!'

'How can he *not* work here? He loves the place, even if it has been altered almost out of all recognition. It's his spiritual home. As a dedicated doctor, he's torn between the knowledge that it's being used for good and the feeling that his heritage has been sacrificed to Mammon. There's a lot of passion beneath that cool exterior, Judith. If I were an American on Skora I'd be half-expecting to parry a blow from his dirk one dark night!'

'You *are* joking?'

Marian smiled. 'Yes, of course. He's more concerned
with saving life than taking it, believe me. Anyway, he
seems to have come to terms with the situation after
three years. Jeffersons have done a lot for Skora and its
people, after all, even if he doesn't care to admit it. Scots
are so proud, aren't they?'

'Wouldn't you say "arrogant" in some cases?' Judith
suggested sweetly.

Marian's glance was shrewd, calculating. 'You must
have caught him on an off day,' she concluded. 'He can
be hard to like at times—and I gather that his love life
isn't running too smoothly just now.'

Judith raised a sardonic eyebrow. 'I'm surprised to
hear that he has one!'

'My dear girl! Didn't you *look* at the man?' It was
light, laughing.

Judith reached for her mug of cocoa. 'Oh, he's attractive—if you like the type,' she conceded coolly.
'Very physical.' It wasn't approving.

'Instant turn-on!'

Judith shrugged. 'Not for me. The reverse in fact—
instant turn-off. I can't stand men who are so full of their
own importance that they can't be bothered to be
reasonably polite. I didn't like him and I certainly don't
fancy him.' It sounded convincing, even to her own ears.
She refused to remember that odd little quiver along her
spine or the strange stirring of an unwelcome excitement
in the secret places of her body.

'Every woman on Skora fancies our Brad and angles
to catch his eye,' Marian declared sweepingly and with
scant regard for truth. 'It seems to be firmly fixed on
Susan Craigie, more's the pity. She has the built-
in advantage of having known him for ever—*and*

she's a doctor. Not much hope for lesser mortals, I'm afraid.'

'Steady girl-friend?' She wasn't really interested, but Marian obviously expected her to make some comment.

'They're virtually engaged. Heaven knows what he sees in her! She's lovely to look at but she's the least favourite person on Skora, by all accounts. No one likes her.'

'It sounds as if they deserve each other,' Judith said, bored.

Marian looked at her curiously. 'You really didn't like him, did you? Tell me—what did our Brad do to put you off so thoroughly? Make a pass?'

'He didn't do anything, exactly. I just didn't take to the man.' It was light and slightly defensive. Judith couldn't have explained even to herself just why the surgeon had set her tingling and filled her with a determination to keep him severely at arms' length. Not that she expected it to be necessary, which only made it all the more absurd, she thought wryly. It had been quite obvious that he neither liked nor approved of her so she wasn't likely to be in any danger from his attentions even if he was more attractive than any man had the right to be. She smiled at Marian. 'There must be other men on Skora and I'm hoping to meet one or two of them, of course. But I'll give it a few days before I start looking!'

'You won't have to look. You'll be falling over them,' Marian said shrewdly. 'The word will soon get round. Actually, it's just as well that you weren't struck all of a heap by Brad Hamilton. That was the trouble with his last theatre nurse. She was madly in love with him and he didn't have an ounce of patience or understanding. He wasn't at all kind to the poor girl and she was forever in floods of tears. She used all the wrong tactics with a man like Brad, of course. He hates sentiment.'

Judith rose to her feet. 'It certainly has no place in an operating theatre,' she said lightly.

Marian laughed. 'I can see that you were made for our resident surgeon. That's just the kind of thing I'd expect to hear on *his* lips! But you aren't going yet?'

'I must—really! I'm dead on my feet and I'm on duty tomorrow morning—in Theatres.' She paused with a hand on the door. 'Is he a good surgeon, by the way?'

Marian shrugged, hesitated. 'I suppose he must be. He doesn't lose his patients on the table and he's very neat with his needle.'

Damned with faint praise, Judith thought as she closed the door of her own apartment. The light words had been faintly tinged with malice and she suddenly realised that her new friend didn't like the surgeon any more than she did. She referred to him as if they were friends. She spoke easily and amusingly of 'fancying' him. But she certainly didn't like him. No doubt she had her reasons.

For her part, she felt that she had good reason to dislike Brad Hamilton. He had made her feel gauche and foolish. He had made her feel unwelcome, an intruder in his native land. Worst crime of all in her book, he didn't seem to appreciate her worth as a Hartlake nurse.

Hartlake was famous for its high standards of training and its jealously-preserved traditions. Its nurses were known and respected and sought-after throughout the world and Judith had worked hard for the small silver badge that was regarded as an open door to the best jobs in the profession. So it infuriated her that an obscure surgeon from the back of beyond should regard her with such indifference.

She didn't care how he felt about her as a person. But he must be made to realise that he was extremely fortunate to have a Hartlake-trained nurse as a member of his team.

Her efficiency and expertise would leave Brad Hamilton gasping with admiration, she determined proudly . . .

Setting out to prove it the very next day, Judith arrived early to familiarise herself with the layout of Theatres and to introduce herself to other members of the team. She was impressed by the unit with its dove-tailing arrangement of changing-rooms and sterilising room and recovery ward and the anaesthetic room and scrub-up annexe directly connected to the spacious operating-room with its array of highly technical and up-to-the-minute equipment. American money and American know-how, she thought, marvelling.

She hadn't expected anything quite so splendid and so sophisticated. If it wasn't for the fly in the ointment that was Brad Hamilton, she could really enjoy the coming months at the Jefferson Clinic. She cautioned herself not to let the man get under her skin. As he had said himself, she didn't have to like him to do a good job.

She knew that she was an efficient instrument nurse, quick and accurate and cool-headed in emergency. She'd had a lot of experience in theatre work and loved it. Working as the surgeon's right hand, she would need her excellent memory for procedures but she was confident that she could anticipate his every need and supply it at just the right moment.

She could organise successfully, too—and that would

be an important part of her duties. She had to ensure that everyone on the team knew exactly what to do and did it. She would carry a lot of responsibility for the smooth running of Theatres but Judith knew that she was equal to it. She certainly didn't mean to allow Brad Hamilton to undermine her confidence.

Begin as you mean to go on, my girl, she told herself firmly, asking brisk questions and issuing necessary instructions to such good effect that staff and Theatres were ready for the surgeon long before he eventually arrived to begin the day's list.

The liking of her new colleagues wasn't so important as their respect for her badge and their prompt obedience to her bidding, Judith decided, not realising that her warm smile took the sting from her coolly formal approach to her work and that her obvious familiarity with the way a theatre should be run was greeted with relief by the team. They were all fed-up with agency nurses with little interest in the job and they had all suffered from the casual inefficiency of the previous theatre nurse with its inevitable effect on a quick-tempered surgeon. So they welcomed the newcomer for her professionalism as well as for her own sake.

The anaesthetist arrived in good time to check his complicated equipment. Rod McNulty was a quiet-spoken Scot in his middle thirties, fair-haired, big-boned and not easy to ruffle. Judith liked him immediately. She liked the strong clasp of his hand and the twinkle in his eyes and the soft voice with its friendly overtones.

He peered at her silver badge. 'Hartlake, is it?' The tone was approving. 'Well, now, we all know that splendid hospital. Fine nurses—and bonny ones, too.' He looked around at the gleaming, orderly theatre with its laid-up trolleys and neat stacks of gowns and masks, the carefully positioned arc lights, its air of quiet readiness. 'It's a pleasure to welcome you to Jefferson,' he said warmly, meaning it.

They talked for a few minutes while he fiddled with tubing and adjusted taps and checked dials. His wife was a community nurse attached to a group practice in Skyllyn, he told her. Judith's ears pricked at the sound of a familiar name.

'Dr Craigie?' she echoed. 'I've heard that name.'

'She's a very good doctor. She may not be well-liked but she knows her medicine.'

Judith nodded. 'Is it the patients who don't like her?'

'She's an autocratic lassie. Gives orders and expects them to be obeyed—and the islanders are independent people. They remember Susan Craigie as a bossy wee girl set on getting her own way and whilst they take great pride in her cleverness they don't take kindly to her manner.' Rod smiled. 'She doesn't send us any patients, by the way. She doesn't approve of private hospitals. The prevention and the treatment and the cure of sickness by the state is every man's right, she says. No doubt she's right, in theory. In practice, the waiting lists are too long and there are never enough hospital beds. In my view, places like this one are supplying a need . . . and shortening the waiting lists for those who can't afford to pay for treatment.'

'What about Dr Sinclair? He's a partner in the same practice, isn't he? Does he share Dr Craigie's views?'

'We have the occasional patient referred by Jamie Sinclair. He's very well-liked by most people on Skora, you'll find. But then, he works at being popular. Susan couldn't care less about being liked. She's a prickly young woman but she earns my respect. If only because she says what she means and means what she says.'

There was something in the quiet words that told Judith that he didn't have that kind of respect for Jamie. She was curious, slightly dismayed. Having plunged into impulsive liking for the friendly, red-headed doctor, she didn't want to find that her usual good judgment had let her down. She remembered that Brad Hamilton had spoken of him with scorn. But there wasn't time to draw the anaesthetist to say more.

'Here comes the big white chief,' Rod said softly, a smile in his voice. 'With a big black devil on his shoulder by the look of him.'

Judith flashed him a swift, laughing glance that immediately established a warm understanding between them. Then she went to greet the surgeon who had chosen just the wrong moment to walk into Theatres. There was no welcoming smile for him as she walked towards him briskly, the shining chignon of fair hair concealed by the theatre cap, her slenderness emphasised by the thin, short-sleeved theatre frock and a hint of challenge in the direct grey eyes.

'Good morning, Mr Hamilton.' It was cool and very formal.

'Good morning . . .' Something that might have been surprise flickered in his dark eyes. For one brief, startled moment, Brad hadn't recognised this mature young woman with the very capable air as the girl of jeans and jersey and flyaway hair that he had rescued in Skyllyn on the previous evening. 'Ready for me?'

He was fifteen minutes later than expected. Judith couldn't resist looking rather pointedly at the clock on the wall. 'Quite ready. You're rather late, sir. Your first patient is on his way up to Theatres. I wondered if we would have to begin without you.' Her tone was light but it was an unmistakable rebuke.

The dark eyes narrowed. Judith knew that he wasn't used to being chided by a mere nurse and resented it. But if she was responsible for Theatres then it was part of her job to see to it that operations began on time if possible. Unless a surgeon was delayed by an emergency then he had no business to be late. It was typical of the arrogance of this man that he felt he could stroll in when it suited him, she thought with a shaft of dislike.

'I don't doubt that you're quite capable of carrying out a simple cholecystectomy but the patient might object,' he said, very dry. 'He's paying a considerable sum of money for my services, you see.' He nodded to Rod McNulty. 'Sorry to have held you up . . . I'll be with you in ten minutes!' About to turn away, he paused. 'You seem to have made a good beginning, Miss Henty. But new brooms do sweep clean, of course. We'll see if you're as efficient after a few weeks—if you last that long.'

As he strode off to change into surgical greens and to scrub-up, Judith sped to put on her sterile theatre gown and mask in readiness to assist. She found that she was seething. Her hands actually shook with the force of her dislike for Brad Hamilton who didn't like or approve of her and showed it all too clearly.

She had been prepared to find that he wasn't as black as weariness and hunger and slight dismay at first sight of Skora had painted him. She had wondered if a defensive kind of antagonism in herself had triggered his hostility. She had been curious to know if he really was as physically attractive as memory insisted. Now she knew that first impressions had been right on all counts. He really was too attractive with those dark eyes and dark, curling hair and the strong good looks—and he really was the most detestable man she had ever met!

She would dearly love to be able to fault his surgical skill, she thought later, watching with a critical eye as he operated. But his hands were swift and very sure and incredibly sensitive and he had a feeling for his work that surprised her. She could compare his technique favourably with any of the fine surgeons at Hartlake and she wondered why he had chosen general surgery in a private clinic in the Highlands instead of making a name for himself in one particular field of surgery in Edinburgh or Glasgow or even London. She didn't doubt that he could have done so. He had the skill and the sensitivity and she realised that he also had the single-minded dedication.

She was reluctantly forced to revise a few of her original ideas about the man. She could forgive such a good surgeon quite a lot, she felt. It pleased her to feel that she could look forward to working with him when she had known so much trepidation about the kind of surgeon he might turn out to be. She hadn't doubted his qualifications, of course. He had all the right letters after his name. She had doubted the extent of his caring. To Judith, that was one of the first essentials for a really first-class surgeon.

He was very neat with his needle as Marian had assured her. Watching as he made the final suture, waiting with poised dish for the discarded instruments, she saw the furrowed brow and the intense concentration in the dark eyes above the green surgical mask.

When the last stitch had been carefully set and the dressing applied and the patient was ready to be transferred to the recovery ward, he straightened his tall frame and stepped back from the table, flexing his gloved hands.

Then, for the first time since receiving the nod from the anaesthetist to proceed, he looked at Judith as though he recognised that she was a person rather than an efficient robot. He gave her a brief nod of approval. 'Thank you, Nurse. You did very well. It makes all the difference to work with someone who really knows her job,' he said levelly.

Judith was surprised by the unexpected praise. She had only carried out a routine task to the best of her ability, after all. But it was nice to know that she had done it to his satisfaction. Not because she liked him as a man and wished to please him, but because she owed it to his skill as a surgeon. She looked up from counting swabs and smiled at him involuntarily, warmth leaping to the grey eyes.

There was no answering smile in the deep-set dark eyes. 'But a little less banter between you and Mr McNulty would be appreciated in future,' he added, spoiling the effect.

'It eases the tension, laddie. You know that,' Rod intervened gently.

'And interferes with my concentration.' It was brusque, uncompromising. He turned away, drawing down his mask.

Judith went on counting swabs, refusing to feel rebuffed and reminding herself that almost every surgeon had some little quirk of temperament or character. She didn't think that the occasional, light remark that had passed between her and the anaesthetist could have disturbed his concentration so much. He hadn't seemed to notice while he was intent on his patient and his work and it certainly hadn't affected her own concentration or her readiness to pass clamp or retractor or swab as needed. He was just being bloody-minded. A smile wouldn't have cost him anything, she thought wryly. They had to work together and it might as well be on outwardly friendly terms, she felt. But Brad Hamilton obviously didn't share that view.

'Take no notice,' Rod said quietly, busily attaching tubes to new cylinders of oxygen and nitrous oxide in preparation for the next patient. 'His bark is worse than his bite.' He adjusted a valve and smiled at her. 'He said himself that it made all the difference having you to assist. That should be some compensation for the sting in the tail.'

Judith looked at him with liking. 'It's all right,' she assured him lightly. 'I won't burst into tears because of a few sharp words. I've had worse thrown at me in my time. There's one surgeon at Hartlake who shall remain nameless who's known as the prima donna because he really loses his cool at the least thing. I can handle a bad-tempered surgeon—especially when he's so good at his job.'

Rod nodded. 'I think you're going to be very good for our Brad. He needs taming and you're just the girl to do it. You'll have him eating out of your hand in no time.'

Judith laughed. 'The impossible I can do right away, thanks to Hartlake. But miracles take a little longer!' she retorted, eyes twinkling.

CHAPTER FOUR

BRAD rolled up his gown and dropped it with his mask into the 'dirty' bin in the ante-room. The glass partition had provided him with an excellent view of the little scene between nurse and anaesthetist. He hadn't been able to hear what was said, of course. But he'd seen the warm glow in her eyes and the effect of that quite enchanting smile on the man who'd moved to her side at the first opportunity.

He frowned.

She was trouble with a capital T. He could sense it. She was much too pretty and she had a great deal of confidence and the kind of feminine appeal that most men would find irresistible. Sinclair had been obviously smitten at first sight. Now, Rod McNulty, happily married and no womaniser, was reacting like any red-blooded male to her allure. It seemed to be unconscious but he suspected that Judith Henty knew just what she was doing when she smiled at a man in that way. She had probably caused havoc among all the impressionable young doctors at Hartlake, he thought grimly.

He was not so young and not easily impressed by a pretty face or a slender, provocative figure with its tiny waist and small, tilting breasts, but even he could respond to her femininity. He was very much a man—and a sensual one at that. But he didn't care for the way his body stirred or the suddenly realised trend of his thoughts as he watched her moving about the theatre, hurrying without haste and checking every detail like a well-trained nurse.

Everyone else had taken time off for a coffee break but she had remained behind to run a careful eye over the trolley, laid-up for the first of the hernia repairs, to check the array of hypodermic syringes and phials of drugs and to ensure that all used gowns and gloves and unsterile equipment had been whisked from the theatre to avoid any risk of cross-infection.

Watching, Brad felt a flicker of amusement that didn't show itself in his expression. She was so determined to prove herself, he thought dryly. Well, that wasn't a bad thing—and he had no fault to find with her so far, except that he didn't take kindly to being addressed as if he were an irresponsible medical student. He had swallowed it that morning, making allowances. Next time, he would put her firmly in her place . . .

She was a marvellous instrument nurse, he admitted fairly—if only to himself. She would be a definite asset to him and he wondered why she had chosen to leave a good job at a famous London hospital to work in the lonely Hebrides. She might last the six months of her contract but he thought it unlikely that she would stay longer. She was too obviously a town girl with town ways and attitudes . . .

Suddenly sensing his gaze, Judith looked directly at the surgeon. Their eyes met and held for a moment. She smiled. Brad Hamilton didn't. Impatience flickered across the very attractive face and then he turned away abruptly. It was unmistakable and almost brutal rebuff.

Judith didn't mind that he'd been watching her so openly. She did mind the feeling that he'd been waiting and hoping to fault her work in some way. How he'd love to point out a mistake or an oversight, she thought, smarting. She was determined not to give him that satisfaction.

Almost before she realised, the last patient on the list was being trundled off to Recovery and she had completed her first day as Brad Hamilton's theatre nurse. It had been busy but rewarding and she had enjoyed her work, despite the surgeon's cool and uncompromising attitude. Everything had gone smoothly and she had got on well with the rest of the team and no one seemed to have noticed his consistent formality where she was concerned. She was already 'Judith' to them all with the easy camaraderie that always existed in Theatres to counteract the tension and the sense of urgency that they all felt during surgery. But he continued to call her 'Nurse' or 'Miss Henty', as though the use of her first name might imply a friendliness he didn't intend to adopt towards her. Well, she could be just as formal, if that was the way he wanted it, she decided proudly—and she certainly wouldn't feel the lack of his liking. He was one person she could do without in her off-duty hours, even if she had to swallow her instinctive dislike and resentment when they were together in Theatres.

Thankfully, she pulled off the cap that had covered her hair all day. As always, the faint smell of ether clung to her skin and hair and clothes, but she was used to that. She changed out of her theatre dress into her own clothes, glad to be going off duty and hoping there would be time to explore the beautiful grounds and perhaps find her way to the sea before dusk fell. It promised to be a fine evening and she could use some fresh air after the long day inside.

Making her way from the building, she was hailed by

Ailsa Macintosh as she passed the open door of the administrator's office.

'Come in for a moment, Miss Henty! I hoped to see you before you went off duty. What sort of a day have you had?' she asked with the warm friendliness that endeared her to all the staff at the clinic.

'No problems,' Judith assured her, smiling. 'One theatre is much like another and routine is pretty standard, of course. I found my feet very quickly.'

'I'm told that you did very well.' Ailsa beamed approval. 'I've just been talking to Mr Hamilton and he was full of praise for your work.'

Judith knew that to be an exaggeration. He wasn't the effusive type. But if he'd been unable to find even the smallest fault for all his critical and uncompromising scrutiny, then she was content. She didn't want more than that from him.

'Well, I enjoyed working with him. Every surgeon develops his own technique and Mr Hamilton is inclined to be rather unorthodox, I found. But he's quick and clever and confident. I think he's a very good surgeon.' It was cool, unemotional—and all the more convincing because she didn't allow her personal dislike of the man to colour her professional view of his ability.

'Passed with flying colours, have I? I'm grateful to you, Miss Henty!' Returning with a remembered question for Ailsa, Brad was just in time to hear the accolade bestowed so generously upon him by his new theatre nurse. He wasn't pleased.

Judith turned at the sardonic words and looked at him levelly, undismayed that he'd overheard, unmoved by the glow of anger in the dark eyes and the grimness of that very sensual mouth.

'I've worked with the best,' she said in her direct way. 'So I think I'm qualified to judge and to voice an opinion.'

'You're not qualified to patronise me,' he returned, quick and angry. 'And I don't give a damn for your opinion! I don't need *you* to tell me that I'm good at my job. I know it, lassie!'

Judith flushed. The familiar Scots term was a whiplash on his lips, harsh and scornful. She'd ruffled his pride— the unforgivable sin, she thought dryly.

'I'm so glad that you decided to be friends, after all,' Ailsa said lightly, making an effort to ease the tension with a little of her dry humour. 'You can afford to be rude to each other! Now, if you *weren't* friends . . .'

Brad gave a short, sharp laugh. 'I'd probably wring her neck!'

Judith smiled reluctantly. For Ailsa's sake, liking the jolly, well-meaning administrator who had the difficult task of keeping the peace between members of the staff who happened to dislike each other. For her own sake, for to be at daggers drawn with the surgeon wouldn't make for a comfortable stay on Skora. She had her own pride but she was prepared to go halfway towards a truce.

'I seem to have offended you. But you weren't meant to hear,' she pointed out reasonably. 'It was a private conversation, after all. I might have been guilty of condescension if I'd said it to your face but I hope I'm not that foolish. I've heard that you have a quick temper,' she added dryly. As if she hadn't just been treated to a taste of it!

'Aye, I can be hasty-tongued.' He didn't smile. He

moved forward to the desk. 'Ailsa, I forgot to ask if you'd managed to reach Sir Geoffrey . . . ?'

Quick to anger, he was equally quick to regret. He'd been too hard on Judith Henty and he ought to apologise, but the words stuck in his throat. He didn't want to give her the least cause to suppose that she'd soon be twisting *him* round her little finger like every other man that she charmed with that lovely smile. He knew the type too well.

There was a hard little lump of hate in Judith's breast as she walked briskly along the corridor to the main door and out into the grounds. She had never felt anything so strongly for anyone in all her life. But she'd never known anyone quite like Brad Hamilton!

She wouldn't let him get her down, she determined fiercely. There were lots of compensations for working with him, fortunately . . .

One of them had left a note for her with Maggie Anderson during the day and Judith read it with a lifting of her spirits. Jamie had been to visit one of his patients and he'd taken the opportunity to remind her of their meeting on the ferry and to give her his telephone number so that she could contact him. The friendly tone of his note warmed the heart that smarted slightly from another man's unexpected and unreasonable antagonism. She was pleased that the personable, good-looking doctor really had carried out his promise to be in touch in the hope of seeing her again. Impulsively, she went to the telephone and put through a call to him.

He was getting ready to take evening surgery at the health centre in Skyllyn and so they could only talk for a few minutes. But it was long enough to make a date for the following day. He was so friendly, so easy to talk to,

that Judith felt she had known him for ever. Because of
Brad Hamilton, she was rather more encouraging than
she might have been, too. She liked the red-headed
doctor and she welcomed his interest in her, in such
contrast to the surgeon's arrogant attitude. She almost
wished it was possible to advertise that friendly and
flattering interest to prove that not every Scot resented
her arrival on Skora!

She rang off, having agreed to meet Jamie for lunch
and a brief tour of the town. As theatre work was
demanding and tiring, it had been sensibly arranged that
she should be off duty on Wednesdays and every
weekend. Judith was pleased with the arrangement and
hoped to enjoy a fairly full social life. The best of the
summer was yet to come, too . . .

Strolling through the narrow streets of Skyllyn with
Jamie the next morning and feeling the barrage of a
hundred curious eyes, Judith realised that everyone
knew everyone else in the small town and took a natural
interest in newcomers. Particularly when the newcomer
was young and female and had the popular Dr Sinclair
for her guide, she thought, amused.

Many of the islanders were his patients and he seemed
to have an excellent memory for names and case histor-
ies and family details. General practice provided plenty
of opportunity for getting to know one's patients really
well, of course, and they tended to regard 'the doctor' as
a family friend. Jamie was obviously well-liked and
respected in the town.

He had a great deal of charm and that easy friendliness
of manner that Judith had found endearing at first
meeting. Although his free time was very precious, he
didn't seem to mind that it was encroached upon by

various people as they made their way towards the
harbour and the hotel where they planned to have lunch.
Just as Rod McNulty had implied, Jamie worked hard at
being liked and Judith found no fault with that. It was
much better than being thoroughly unpleasant for the
hell of it, she decided, her thoughts winging quite involuntarily to Brad Hamilton. It was hard to believe that
he could be popular with his patients or anyone else.

Some time later, she wasn't too pleased to see the
surgeon, but it seemed that social venues were rather
limited on Skora and he happened to be lunching in the
same hotel.

Judith had no trouble at all in identifying his beautiful
companion even before Jamie pointed out his partner in
general practice and took her across to be introduced.
Susan Craigie was exactly as she had imagined. Very
lovely, very self-possessed, very well-dressed and not
very interested in a newcomer who was only a nurse. She
acknowledged the introduction with a cool little smile
and went on eating melon.

There was coolness all round, in fact. Brad Hamilton
scarcely replied to Jamie's friendly greeting and allowed
Judith only the fraction of an unsmiling nod. Icily
annoyed, she wondered why Jamie had dragged her the
width of the hotel dining-room to talk to people who
obviously weren't interested and disliked the interrup-
tion to their tête-á-tête. She was very careful not to smile
at the surgeon.

'I've just been showing Judith something of the town,'
Jamie declared lightly, seemingly unaware of the cool
atmosphere. Judith was forcibly reminded of a friendly
puppy who didn't know that he'd just been snubbed with
a well-aimed toe. 'You remember that I mentioned

meeting Brad's new theatre nurse on the ferry, I dare-say, Susan?'

'I believe you did say something to that effect,' Susan agreed indifferently, betraying that she didn't always listen very attentively to his retailing of local gossip. She looked at Judith, assessing her looks and youth and the inexpensive floral suit she wore, without approval. 'I expect you'll find the Jefferson Clinic very different from your teaching hospital, Miss Henty.' Her tone implied that it was the less dedicated nurses who chose private nursing for the better pay and hours that it offered. She didn't wait for an answer. 'If I'm to do your calls as well as my own this afternoon, then I'll be grateful for the chance to enjoy my lunch, Jamie,' she said pointedly.

Judith was slightly shocked—and not at all surprised. One glance had told her that Susan Craigie didn't care for anyone's opinion and certainly not for their feelings. The 'please or offend' type who invariably offended, she thought dryly. She and Brad Hamilton were *very* well suited!

The surgeon said smoothly: 'Perhaps you and Miss Henty would care to join us, Sinclair? We're only on the first course and we've scarcely touched the wine. Sit down and make it a foursome.'

Judith wasn't sure if he was just being bloody-minded or if he felt that his companion's discourtesy had gone beyond the acceptable even between friends and he ought to make some effort to atone. She glanced quickly at Jamie, willing him to murmur some polite excuse and whisk her away to another table. To her dismay, he either didn't understand or ignored the unspoken mes-sage.

'That's uncommonly decent of you, old man,' he

drawled lightly, in fairly good imitation of public school accents, promptly drawing out a chair for Judith.

She had no option but to subside into it with as good a grace as she could muster. Meeting the surgeon's dark eyes, she found slightly sardonic amusement in their depths and knew that he was delighting in her discomfiture. She didn't want to eat with him and his horrid girl-friend and she didn't doubt that it was showing. But she would have to make an effort or be as guilty of bad manners as Susan Craigie, she realised reluctantly.

But what on earth had possessed Jamie to accept the invitation after such an obvious snub from his partner? She stifled the unworthy thought that he'd angled for the opportunity to join them. He couldn't have wanted to intrude on their privacy—or spoil her enjoyment of these few hours in his company!

In all fairness, Jamie didn't know how she felt about Brad Hamilton, she reminded herself. She had carefully avoided the man's name and he hadn't once asked how she'd got on with the surgeon, although he knew that she'd been working with him on her very first day at the Jefferson Clinic. Judith had the very definite impression that there was no love lost between the two men.

Which really made it all the more surprising that he'd chosen that particular moment to introduce her to Susan Craigie. That was one pleasure that could have been postponed indefinitely, Judith thought dryly.

There were very few people that she'd met and hadn't liked or found it easy to get on with. Within days of setting foot on Skora, she'd added two to that very small list!

Brad nodded to a waiter who hastened to set cutlery and bring extra glasses. Judith found herself sipping a very palatable white wine and toying with food for which she no longer had any appetite. Jamie was being the life and soul of the party and she envied his light-hearted indifference to atmosphere. Susan Craigie was looking bored and the surgeon was obviously not listening while Jamie regaled them with the story of his encounter in the High Street with an obviously healthy patient who had shambled into surgery earlier that morning to plead that he was near to death and unfit for work. It wasn't a rare experience. Jamie was recounting the man's total lack of embarrassment as he came up to greet him, telling the tale with a great deal of humour that failed to bring even the glimmer of a smile to his partner's frosty blue eyes.

Judith fumed, wishing she had enough courage to get up and walk away from the embarrassment of this encounter with the surgeon and his girl-friend. But Jamie had placed her in this intolerable situation and he was the only one who could rescue her from it. He just didn't seem to notice her constrained and uncomfortable silence.

'I'm afraid the fish isn't to your liking, Miss Henty. Allow me to order something else for you,' Brad said abruptly.

Judith laid down her fork. 'No, thank you. I'm really not hungry . . .'

'More wine?' He reached for the bottle. It was almost empty and he nodded to the hovering waiter who scurried away to procure another bottle.

She allowed him to refill her glass although she didn't want the wine. It was easier to accept than to protest.

'Wishing me at the bottom of the sea, aren't you?' he murmured, so that only she could hear him.

'Frankly, yes.' Judith saw no reason to be polite or to

pretend. He wasn't trying to conceal his animosity towards her, after all. Heaven knew why he had issued that invitation when he was so obviously not a man of impulse. Judith suspected that she wouldn't really want to know his motives.

'It's a tight community on Skora. We'll be thrust into each other's company on numerous occasions, like it or not,' he told her bluntly.

'I won't like it,' she said sweetly.

He shrugged.

Judith drank some of her wine and turned her head to listen to the end of Jamie's light-hearted account. She turned her shoulder slightly, too.

Brad studied her thoughtfully. She had banded the long, shining hair about her head in an unusual and very sophisticated style that suited her pretty face. Dispassionately, he admired the delicate profile of slender nose and sculpted cheekbone and arch of slanted eyebrow and tilt of slightly stubborn chin. His gaze rested briefly on the thrust of tilting breasts beneath the clinging silk of her blouse. Unexpectedly, his body stirred with the beginnings of desire.

He could understand just why Sinclair was in such hot pursuit and not caring who knew it. In other circumstances, he would be very tempted to coax her into bed himself, he thought—and doubted that she would need much coaxing. Judith Henty was no virgin for all that enchanting air of innocence that was a challenge to any man's sensuality, he decided. She knew exactly what she was doing when she encouraged a man to want her with the promise in her lovely smile and the allure in every line of her beautiful body.

It was rather a pity that she was so obviously a flirt and

very likely a wanton, Brad thought ruefully. He couldn't afford to tangle with that kind of woman. Not even for the duration of a brief but possibly very satisfying affair. For one thing, he was a Hamilton and owed much to his family name and traditions. For another, a surgeon needed to guard his reputation even more carefully than a general practitioner.

But it didn't stop him from wanting her, he admitted. She was a very attractive girl . . .

For Jamie's sake, Judith made an effort. Carefully avoiding any direct speech with the surgeon, she eased her way into the conversation. She asked all the right questions and talked freely about herself and by the end of lunch she fancied that Susan Craigie was thawing slightly. No doubt she hadn't been any better pleased than herself that a tête-à-tête had abruptly become a foursome and Judith wondered if it had been a deliberate strategy on Brad Hamilton's part. They were rumoured to be virtually engaged and perhaps Susan had been hoping to convert rumour into fact over their lunch. If he wasn't too keen to commit himself just yet, he might have welcomed an opportunity to shelve the subject, Judith thought shrewdly.

There was certainly nothing of the lover in the way he looked or smiled or spoke. Marian had said that he hated sentiment and Judith could believe it, studying him and listening to him and marvelling that he was rumoured to be on the point of marrying the beautiful doctor. She was glad that she didn't stand in those very elegant shoes! Brad Hamilton was so cold and dour and obviously unfeeling that she would be sorry for any woman he married. If she loved him.

But it was hard to believe that they loved each other.

Susan Craigie didn't seem the type to inspire love for all her beauty and crisp intelligence. Marian had said that they'd known each other for years and perhaps they'd just drifted into a near-engagement, or maybe Susan had made up her mind to marry him and cleverly manoeuvred him into a situation where everyone expected them to wed. No doubt she must seem a very suitable wife for a successful surgeon who had little time for sentiment, too.

She was exceptionally lovely with that rich abundance of red-gold hair coiled on a slender neck and a magnolia skin and expressive blue eyes in a perfect oval face. Her elegant suit was a very expensive classic and so was the pure silk shirt and the soft leather of matching shoes and bag. She exuded confidence and cool sophistication and she was undoubtedly clever. But she wasn't easy to like, Judith agreed. She was much too sure of herself. She was cold and proud and very self-sufficient and slightly scornful.

They would make a fine pair if they married. A remarkably handsome couple who'd freeze each other to death in no time, Judith thought with a slight shiver.

She didn't like Brad Hamilton and she had no interest whatsoever in his future. So it was really rather absurd to feel that he deserved rather better than Susan Craigie for a wife . . .

CHAPTER FIVE

'THAT wasn't too successful, I'm afraid,' Jamie said ruefully, taking her hand and drawing it through his arm as they left the hotel that overlooked the picturesque harbour of Skyllyn. 'I wanted you to know Susan but she wasn't at her best. I think we must have chosen the wrong moment to join them.'

'We didn't have to eat with them. You could easily have made an excuse,' Judith pointed out in her direct way.

'Yes. I didn't think very quickly, did I? Actually, I didn't realise that Susan was quite so prickly.'

'She was very rude.'

'Oh, not really! That's just her way,' he defended lightly. 'She doesn't beat about the bush.'

'And he doesn't put himself out to be pleasant. You have some delightful friends,' she said dryly.

Jamie laughed. 'Oh, you'll like Susan when you know her better,' he prophesied confidently. 'She's really a great girl. But she isn't at her best with strangers—or when Hamilton's around, I must admit. He seems to cramp her style.'

'That air of silent disapproval would cramp anyone's style!'

'I thought women liked the strong, silent type,' he teased. 'All good looks and brooding passion.'

'Not this woman.'

'That's reassuring.' Jamie covered her slender fingers

as they lay lightly on his arm. The blue eyes danced with a hint of mischief as he looked down at her. 'How do you rate doctors who talk too much?'

'Much to be preferred!' Judith declared, smiling up at him with warmth.

They walked along by the harbour wall, as easy with each other as if they were long-time friends. Judith was interested in watching the fishermen who were mending their nets in readiness to sail on the evening tide. Jamie knew many of them by name. She was pleased that he was so well-liked. She liked him herself and it was nice to feel that they would probably see much of each other in the coming months.

It was much too soon to be thinking of a serious relationship, she knew. But at twenty-three, it was very natural that her thoughts should turn to husband and home in the not-too-distant future. She enjoyed nursing but she didn't want to dedicate the rest of her life to it. Like any girl, she cherished a dream of falling in love and being loved in return. Like any girl, she wanted to be married. Someone like Jamie would suit her very well, she decided impulsively, warming to him.

Nurses made good wives and mothers as a result of their training combined with the qualities that had taken them into nursing in the first place. They made the best possible wives for doctors, too. They knew and understood and accepted the many demands of the medical profession and they had common ground on which to build a good and lasting marriage. Judith firmly believed that physical attraction wasn't the right foundation for a relationship unless it was backed by mutual liking and similar tastes and backgrounds.

Jamie was very presentable and very personable and

she imagined that his easy-going attitude and his light-hearted approach to life would make him an ideal husband for any woman. He was kind and thoughtful and fun and so easy to know that she felt he would be very easy to love, too. But that was moving much too quickly . . .

Judith reined in her thoughts, chiding herself for equating friendship with romance so soon after her first meeting with the good-looking doctor with the red hair and smiling blue eyes. Surely she'd outgrown that sort of thing years ago! Tumbling into love was for teenagers and she'd never believed in love at first sight, anyway.

She certainly wasn't as sure about the feelings that Jamie inspired as she was about the instinctive dislike that she'd felt for Brad Hamilton almost on sight. That was very real and growing with every encounter.

It was unfortunate that he'd intruded into her day with Jamie. It was not of his doing, she admitted fairly. But, thinking of the very uncomfortable hour that they'd spent with the surgeon and his girl-friend, Judith found that she was still throbbing with angry resentment at his attitude.

He hadn't even tried to be friendly. He'd been scarcely polite. He'd allowed Jamie and Susan to do most of the talking, studying them with a sardonic gleam in his dark eyes and taking very little notice of her after that brief exchange. It would be quite unreasonable to expect him to like her when she didn't like him, of course. But he didn't have to make it so obvious to everyone else, Judith thought, smarting.

He'd smiled across the table at Susan in response to some remark and Judith had been startled by the unexpected warmth that leaped to his handsome face and the glow in the deep-set eyes that were a very dark blue rather than the black she had first supposed. In that moment, she had realised the impact of the charm that other people had assured her he possessed in full measure. Then, meeting her eyes, the smile was swept away as though it had never been there.

Foolishly, she had felt the rebuff like a blow. She had blinked in dismay at the extent of his hostility, so unaccountable and so unjustified. Then she had looked back at him with cool eyes and a little tilt to her chin. He had smiled. A very different kind of smile that made her long to slap his face. Cold, mocking, arrogant. As their eyes locked for that tense moment, she'd felt that odd tingling in her spine all over again.

'They're engaged, aren't they?' She heard herself put the impulsive question to Jamie with some surprise. She hadn't meant to show so much interest in the surgeon or his personal affairs.

'Brad and Susan?' Jamie shook his head. 'That's just gossip. She'll never marry him. She knows him much too well.' It was emphatic.

'That can be an advantage, surely?'

'Sometimes . . . when a woman likes all the things she knows about a man. But there are traits in Brad Hamilton that Susan would hesitate to pass on to any children they might have, I'm afraid.' It was sombre in tone and in stark contrast to his usual lightness of manner.

Something very like apprehension shivered down Judith's spine. She recalled the vague feeling of distrust that the surgeon had evoked on first meeting. She remembered that Ailsa Macintosh had described him as 'temperamental' and then suddenly seemed reluctant to say more. She remembered her conviction that Marian didn't really like or trust Brad Hamilton. She thought of Jamie's description—'a man of brooding passions'—and wondered if it had been meant as a gentle warning. She completely forgot the reassuring warmth and kindliness that had dawned in the dark eyes and transformed the lean and very attractive face when he smiled so affectionately at Susan Craigie.

'I'm told that he's very quick-tempered,' she said tentatively, very curious to know what Jamie could mean by those quiet words with their hint of menace.

Jamie hesitated, as though he felt that he might already have said too much. Then he said with a hint of reluctance: 'It's rather more than that, Judith. There's a history of instability in his branch of the family.'

Judith stared, chilled. 'Mental instability?'

'To some extent. Although it's never put into so many words, of course. One merely hears rumours of bad blood in Brad Hamilton. For the most part, the islanders close ranks to protect one of their own.'

'I can't believe it!' Instinctively, Judith rejected the idea. It was too horrid to accept—and there was no way that she was going to believe that a clever and competent and obviously caring surgeon was unstable. Unreasonable and unpredictable—yes! But quite as sane as any person she had ever met!

Jamie drew her down to sit on the harbour wall by his side. His good-looking, rather boyish face was unusually solemn. 'Well, his mother died in mysterious circumstances and his father shot himself soon afterwards, apparently. Brad and his sister Catriona were brought up by their uncle, the laird. It seems they were always a difficult pair. Self-willed, moody, hating to be thwarted and ruled by their passions.' He paused briefly. Then, without emotion, he went on: 'A few years ago, Catriona took an overdose. Not enough to kill herself but enough to scare the hell out of everyone. As a medical student, she knew just how to judge it to a nicety.'

'But that's dreadful!' Judith exclaimed.

Jamie nodded. 'Very sad.'

It was slightly too cool. For some reason, Judith didn't think that he really felt the sentiment and something in his tone jarred on her. 'Why did she do it? Does anyone know?'

'She had a breakdown.' It was slightly cagey. Judith sensed that there was more to Catriona Hamilton's story than he was prepared to tell. She wondered if he regretted having mentioned the girl. 'Failed her exams and couldn't cope with disappointment. No self-control, you see. It's the family flaw. It's more marked in Brad, unfortunately. His temper has got him into trouble on various occasions. Nearly throttling a boy at boarding school, running down a fellow student with his car at university—that kind of thing. Accidents, according to the family. Hushed up to protect the pride of the Hamiltons, according to others.'

'He sounds like a dangerous man,' Judith said quietly, rather doubtfully. She wondered why Jamie was telling her these things. To warn her against getting involved with Brad Hamilton? To put himself in a better light because of the competition in the surgeon's looks and charm that won him any woman he wanted, according to Marian?

'He's a clever one. He always gets away with it,' Jamie retorted. 'Like that business with his cousin . . .' He broke off, shrugging.

'Oh?' Judith prompted, knowing that he meant to say more, despite the pretence of hesitation.

He looked at her thoughtfully. 'You'll think I'm maligning the man, but anyone will tell you the same things about him, Judith. I'd prefer to say nothing, but you'll be working closely with Brad and seeing a lot of him and it's best that you should know the kind of man he is.'

'Yes, of course,' she agreed flatly. She wondered if nurses didn't stay long at the Jefferson Clinic because of Brad Hamilton's quick temper and uncertain behaviour. Then, doubtful, she wondered if that was merely the impression that Jamie wanted to convey—and why!

The doctor folded his arms across his chest and stared out to sea with a frown in his blue eyes. 'Fergus was the laird's only son, heir to everything. There was less than a year between the cousins and they got on well enough until they reached their teens and began to run after the local girls. Then they scrapped a few times over wanting the same girl. Nothing unusual in that, of course. Some years later, Fergus got engaged. A few days after it was announced, the two men went out to sea on one of their regular fishing trips—and only Brad came back. Local fishermen found him clinging to the capsized boat and no sign of Fergus. It was never satisfactorily explained, apparently. But there was talk of an argument over the girl that led to a fight and the boat turning turtle. Another of Brad's "accidents" resulting from a sudden loss of temper? No one really knows. Except Brad—and he won't talk about it.'

'I don't think I want to hear any more,' Judith said quietly.

Jamie put an arm about her shoulders. 'I hope you

aren't upset,' he said swiftly, contrite, 'I didn't think you liked Brad!'

'I don't!'

'Women do,' he remarked, very light. 'He has rather an unsavoury reputation on that score, too, I'm afraid.'

The scales were weighed so heavily against the surgeon who wasn't there to defend himself that Judith felt bound to protest. 'It can't be that bad or he wouldn't remain on the medical register!'

'I only mean that he likes the women. To the best of my knowledge, he's never been involved in a scandal that attracted the interest of the BMA.' Jamie said smoothly.

It was slightly too smooth. Earlier, he hadn't shown any sign of disliking the surgeon so much or having so little good to say about him. But she didn't really want to think that he was devious and she was troubled. 'I suppose you've known him for years?'

'Only since I came to work on Skora, three years ago. To be frank, we don't get on. Susan and I are good friends and he's just a little jealous.' He smiled. 'Needlessly so, of course. There's only one man for Susan.'

There was the merest edge to his tone. Judith didn't notice. 'I thought you were an islander,' she said in surprise.

'Did you? I'm from Edinburgh. But Skora is a grand place and everyone has made me feel at home here. I know they'll do the same for you.' He reached for her hand and squeezed it confidently.

She smiled, rather doubtfully. It was true that almost everyone she'd met so far had been friendly and welcoming. But most of them had been from the mainland, like herself. She had a strong suspicion that the natives of

Skora were proud and reserved people who didn't really welcome newcomers. Both Brad Hamilton and Susan Craigie had shown that very plainly!

'I suppose three years is long enough to get to know someone really well,' she said quietly. Six months of almost daily contact with the surgeon should teach her all she wanted to know, she thought wryly. It would probably be the hardest six months of her life.

Jamie shrugged. 'It is on Skora. We see so much of each other and someone like Brad is always providing food for gossip in one way or another. I've heard most of his history from Susan, actually—and I don't think she can be accused of gossiping. I think she just needed to talk to an outsider about the way she feels about him. She loves him but she doesn't think it wise to marry him. It isn't easy for the poor girl.'

It couldn't be easy for Brad Hamilton, either, Judith thought on a surge of compassion. Perversely, in view of her dislike of him and all that she had just heard about him, she felt sorry for him. It must be dreadful to live with such a past. One didn't have to like someone to feel sympathy and concern if his life had been shadowed by a series of tragic events—and if Brad Hamilton really had been responsible for some of them, then it must be hell to live with that burden of guilt and in the shadow of a quick temper that might too easily lead to further tragedy.

No wonder he was so cold and remote, so detached and dispassionate, so disinclined to become involved in any way with a newcomer. It seemed that he could only relax with someone like Susan who loved him. Perhaps he couldn't afford to loosen the tight rein on emotions that were apparently such a threat to himself and to

others. It might be one of the reasons why he continued
to live and work on Skora when he could have furthered
his career very successfully on the mainland, she thought
with sudden insight. Here, he was known and accepted
and loved, despite his history. Here, he was surrounded
by friendship and affection even if he'd lost his home and
his heritage. Here, he was doing the work that he
obviously loved and doing it well and he hadn't had to
sacrifice friends and family and familiar surroundings as
she had. Instead of feeling sorry for him, perhaps she
ought to be envious, Judith thought dryly . . .

Jamie drove her back to Skelbeg and the clinic that
evening. As he had to get back in time for evening
surgery, she persuaded him to drop her at the main
gates. The short walk through the grounds would only
take a few minutes and it was a fine evening.

'It won't take a moment to run you up to the annexe,'
Jamie said, slowing the car as they approached the
gateway. But he glanced at his watch as he spoke.

Judith shook her head. He'd given her more than
enough of his time that day. 'I haven't yet had a chance
to explore the grounds and this is a good opportunity,'
she assured him lightly. She smiled at him. 'It's been a
lovely day, Jamie. I've really enjoyed it.'

'The first of many,' he said confidently.

'Why not?'

He leaned to kiss her, very lightly, the merest brush of
his lips. She touched her hand to his smooth cheek in an
impulsive gesture of affection and then drew away.
Neither of them wanted more at this stage. Both of them
felt that they were on the verge of more than ordinary
friendship. But there was no need to rush into anything.

'Sunday . . . ?' He opened the car door.

'Sunday,' she confirmed, smiling.

She waved as the car drove off towards Skyllyn and then began to walk along the tree-lined drive. It had been a pleasant day and she'd enjoyed Jamie's company.

He hadn't referred again to the surgeon and she wondered if he felt that he'd said too much to his detriment. None of it had been actively malicious, Judith decided in retrospect. Yet she couldn't rid herself of the faint suspicion that he didn't want her to like Brad Hamilton. There was little risk of that, she thought dryly. They'd already clashed so many times that it was obvious that they would never be friends.

Rounding a corner, she paused to admire the old house in its gracious setting. The roseate glow of the sunset was touching the old stone walls and reflecting in the long windows. Very sensitive to beauty, Judith caught her breath in delight and wished she'd known Hamilton House in the days when it had been a much-loved home. Even now, it had an aura of peace and warmth and tranquillity that seemed to make a nonsense of Jamie's lurid hints. It was hard to believe in dark passions or to accept the declaration that there was a streak of madness in the family. It was simply the kind of thing that people liked to invent about ancient families, she decided sensibly.

It would be interesting to know more about the long line of Hamiltons who'd lived and loved through the years on Skora. She had been fascinated by the family portraits that still adorned the first-floor gallery and she was looking forward to a closer study. She wondered if all the Hamilton men had been as proud and as passion-ate as Brad with his quick temper and unfortunate past—and if all the women had been as emotional and easily overcome by disappointment as the unknown Catriona. It was almost a pity that the surgeon was so unfriendly for she would have loved to hear all about the house and the Hamilton history and the family legends from someone so closely concerned.

Gazing at the house, lost in reverie, Judith was suddenly aware with that odd and uncomfortable prickling of the hair on the nape of her neck that she was being observed. She swung round, instantly on the defensive.

The surgeon stood in the shadow of the trees, regarding her intently, dark eyes glittering in the bronzed, handsome face. Tall and broad and impressive in the formal grey suit, he was so attractive that in different circumstances her pulses might have leaped for another reason than apprehension. But with her head abruptly full of all that Jamie had said and hinted about Brad Hamilton, she froze with sudden and unreasonable panic. He saw her as an invader, some kind of threat, she felt. He would drive her from Skora if he could—and she fancied that he wouldn't be too scrupulous about the methods he used!

He moved towards her and a shiver of alarm rippled down her spine. She stiffened but she stood her ground despite an absurd desire to run from him as fast as her feet would carry her. There was something about the too-attractive surgeon that unnerved her, set her tingling in every vein, quickened a strange kind of unwelcome excitement. But she didn't mean him to know it!

'Turned to stone, Miss Henty?' he drawled, mocking.

She wondered how long he'd stood beneath the trees, watching her, while she contemplated the house and thought about him and his family. 'I was admiring the house,' she said, rather defensively. 'I like old houses.

This one is very lovely.' She saw the dark eyes narrow and harden as though he resented a stranger's interest in the heritage of the Hamiltons. He was so proud and so suspicious that he probably thought it was insincere patronisation! 'It must mean a great deal to you,' she added. An angel rushing in where even fools would fear to tread, she thought wryly.

'You are mistaken,' he said brusquely, without emotion. 'I'm not the kind of man to waste time and energy on caring for something I shall never possess.'

She didn't believe him. Wisely, she didn't say so. She began to walk on and he fell into step by her side. 'I didn't expect to see you again today,' she said, light and cool, carefully friendly. She even managed a smile rather than let him suspect that she was uneasy in his company.

Brad's dark brows snapped together abruptly. He had no intention of responding to the golden warmth of her smile and the unmistakable hint of coquetry in her manner. Girls like this one didn't need that kind of encouragement, he thought with a flicker of contempt. She might make fools of other men, but he wasn't an easy victim for her kind. His body might stir with unaccountable and rather disturbing desire for a stranger but his mind and heart could view her with indifferent scorn.

'Why should you? I'm not usually around at this hour,' he said levelly. 'I decided to have another look at Mr Mallory. I'm not too happy about that chest infection.'

'I wish I'd known you were coming back this evening. You could have given me a lift. Jamie was rather rushed for time.' It was careless, not meant, merely an attempt to make slightly stilted conversation with the man who strode by her side, disdain and discouragement written all over his handsome face.

'Aye, I could have brought you,' he agreed, without warmth. 'If I'd wished for your company . . .'

That should leave her in no doubt that casting out lures to him was a complete waste of time, he thought dryly . . .

CHAPTER SIX

Colour flew into Judith's face and she was hot with anger as well as dismayed by the unmistakable and quite unnecessary snub. Her fingers itched to slap the lean, sensual face with its stamp of arrogance. She smarted at the implication that he suspected her of trying to flirt with him. Damn the man—*and* the good looks that had apparently tempted so many women to make a bid for his interest that he'd become puffed up with conceit and contemptuous of her sex!

She couldn't be blind or entirely immune to the potency of his physical attractions, but it didn't mean that she liked him or wanted anything more than a strictly professional involvement with him. And she fiercely resented his obvious assumption that she did!

She stopped short, glowering. 'I don't want to see any more of *you* than I have to, either,' she said coldly.

Brad shrugged. 'Then we both know where we stand.' It was light, indifferent. He regarded her with a hint of amusement, liking her sudden show of spirit. She wasn't afraid to cross swords with him and she obviously didn't give a snap of her fingers for his liking or approval even if it was second nature for her to smile and flutter those long lashes in meaningless invitation.

There were some qualities in Judith Henty that compelled his reluctant admiration. But having seen her in action with Sinclair and Rod McNulty as well as himself in the few days since her arrival on Skora, he was reminded too forcibly of another pretty flirt who'd done irrevocable damage to his life.

Judith was too angry to notice the little smile in the depths of his dark eyes—and if she had, it would only have served to increase rather than allay her indignation.

With an effort, she choked back hot words that would only worsen the situation and make it quite impossible for them to go on working together. She liked her job at the Jefferson Clinic and she wanted to keep it, despite the necessary evil of working with this detestable brute of a man. The one redeeming factor was his undeniable ability as a surgeon. They made a splendid surgical team, his skill and her Hartlake training complementing each other perfectly, so what did it matter that outside Theatres they simply couldn't get on? They could ensure that their paths didn't cross too often, after all.

'This is ridiculous,' she said, very cool, very much on her dignity. 'I refuse to quarrel with you, Mr Hamilton. You've been as unpleasant as you can be in the last few days and it's obvious that you don't want me here. But I'm staying. I've not the slightest intention of giving up an interesting and rewarding job just to please you!'

He raised an eyebrow. 'But it wouldn't please me if you left,' he said levelly. 'For all your faults, you're an excellent theatre nurse.'

'*Damn you!*' she flared, furious. 'For all *my* faults, indeed! Would you like me to catalogue a few of yours? It would take too long to list them all, heaven knows! But I could begin with your intolerable rudeness and your insufferable arrogance and . . .' She broke off, breast heaving, as she realised that he was laughing at her. There was unmistakable amusement in the dancing dark eyes and a sudden warmth of expression transformed him from dour Scot to human and likeable and very attractive male in a moment. Judith glowered, despite the unexpected impact on her senses of the man's physical magnetism. How dare he add insult to injury by greeting her perfectly justified anger with amusement!

'Very wise of you not to quarrel with me, Miss Henty,' he said, eyes twinkling. 'One can only admire your restraint.'

Her chin tilted. 'You're impossible!' she declared icily, resisting the impulse to laugh with him, and turned away.

In two strides, he caught her up and his hand came down hard on her shoulder. 'Hold on!' he exclaimed. 'We can't go on like this, you know. I don't know who declared this war but it's about time we called a truce!'

Judith wasn't prepared for the way that he smiled or the electric shock that sped down her spine at his touch. The warmth and attraction of the smile that softened the rather harsh planes of his handsome face took her by surprise. So did her body's reaction to that hand on her shoulder. Alarmed and suspicious and still angry, she didn't trust the charm of that smile or the sudden volte-face of his attitude. She didn't smile back at him. She was rigid with dislike and distrust.

She shook his hand from her shoulder. 'Go to hell,' she said, clear and concise.

His smile deepened. 'I'm afraid we didn't get off to a very good start,' he said quietly, regarding her with thoughtful eyes.

Judith bridled. 'Well, that wasn't *my* fault! I don't know why you've been so unfriendly!' The words spilled before she could check them, indignant and accusing and reproachful. The injustice of his behaviour ever since they'd met had suddenly welled up in her breast. He didn't have to like her but she hadn't done anything to deserve the way he'd looked and spoken and failed to smile . . . until now. And now was too late, she thought angrily.

She'd seen too much of Brad Hamilton's true nature to be charmed just because he'd suddenly decided for reasons of his own that it was time to be nice to her!

Looking down at her, observing the warmth in her face and the militant sparkle in the grey eyes, Brad was suddenly and disturbingly aware of her as a woman. The quickened rise and fall of small, taut breasts beneath the thin silk blouse set the fire leaping in his loins and he was amazed by the strength and the ardour of a need that she evoked so swiftly in him.

'I'm a canny Scot, I suppose,' he said slowly. 'I don't rush into liking every Tom, Dick or Harriet who walks into my life. Nor should you.' He detained her with a firm hand on her arm as she turned away, suddenly too impatient to listen to him. 'I've already told you that you're too trusting, Judith. You'll not heed the warning but you'll be wise to avoid getting too involved with Sinclair. He isn't a man to trust.' He knew he was wasting his breath by the way she stiffened.

Judith didn't know that his body was on fire for her but she sensed the tumult and tension in his tall frame and she was suddenly apprehensive. She felt oddly threatened by the look in his dark eyes and her heart began to thump and foolish thoughts crowded into her mind. It was dusk but there were plenty of people within hearing and it wasn't so very secluded where they stood among the trees. She wasn't afraid of him. That was absurd! She was merely much too aware of his magnetism as his gaze held her own and he stood rather too close for comfort.

She was tingling from head to toe. Not at his touch, she denied strenuously, but with fury that he should speak ill of someone like Jamie. She was so angry that she didn't even notice that he'd used her first name with quiet and friendly familiarity.

She whisked her arm from his hand as though he'd scorched her flesh. 'And you *are*? That isn't the way I hear it!' It was quick, scornful.

The smile fled from his eyes. Just as he'd suspected, Sinclair had been spilling his particular brand of poison and she had been only too ready to believe all that she'd heard. 'Then you must make up your mind which of us to believe.'

'I have!' she declared, very pointed.

Brad studied her thoughtfully. 'What has he told you? That I killed my cousin?'

It was quiet, matter-of-fact. But Judith saw that he was very angry. His hands had clenched and a nerve throbbed in his lean cheek. 'No!' It was swift denial. But her face was suddenly suffused with conscious warmth.

'Not in so many words? He's aye clever,' he said, sardonic.

'He told me there'd been a boating accident . . .' She broke off at the sudden blaze in his dark eyes.

'The man has a way of presenting the truth in the worst possible light,' Brad commented grimly, struggling for control. There'd been many a time when he'd have killed the man with his bare hands if he hadn't learned to keep a tight rein on his dangerous temper. There seemed to be no other way to silence him at such times. Fortunately, his friends stood by him no matter what Sinclair said to blacken his name. It was unfortunate that Judith Henty was so ready to believe the worst of him, but it didn't really matter. Her good opinion was of very little importance, after all. His mouth tightened abruptly. 'I don't have to defend myself to you, damn it!' He strode away from her, stiff with pride.

Judith looked after him, torn between the stubborn distrust of him and an odd desire to believe that he couldn't be quite as black as Jamie had painted him.

Unexpectedly, he turned and came back to her with swift, determined strides. 'Well, the man's got it right,' he said harshly. 'I did kill Fergus.'

Heart seeming to stop with the shock of the admission, Judith caught her breath. Then she shook her head in instinctive rejection. 'It was an accident,' she heard herself saying with quiet and steadfast conviction. 'It couldn't have been anything else.' Whatever Brad Hamilton might be, he wasn't the kind of man to take life. He worked too hard to preserve and improve on it.

She was moved by the memory of anguish that was etched so sharply on the handsome features. Suddenly, without rhyme or reason, she wanted to put her arms about him and hold him to drive away the devil that still tormented him in heart and mind. He'd been to hell and back, she thought with swift compassion.

He looked at her for a long, tense moment. 'Thank you,' he said, very brusque. Then he left her and this time he didn't turn back.

Judith discovered that she was trembling. It had been a strange encounter with a very strange man, she thought wryly. She hadn't been exactly frightened of him but he had alarmed her in some deep and inexplicable way.

She almost ran the last few yards to the annexe, meeting Marian on her way from the day's duty as she reached the building.

The dark-haired girl eyed her breathless condition with some concern. 'What's wrong? Were you frightened by our prowler?' She turned to look along the rather secluded path that Judith had used in order to skirt the house and shorten her route.

'What prowler?' She felt uneasy.

'Someone's been lurking in the grounds, apparently. He hasn't actually done anything, but he's alarmed a few of the girls and people are getting nervous of walking on their own after dark. It's probably just one of the village lads playing silly pranks—or a peeping Tom. Make sure that you draw your curtains at night, won't you?'

Judith shivered. 'And I thought Skora was such a peaceful place!' she exclaimed with a wry laugh. 'No, I didn't see anything suspicious. I've just been hurrying.'

She didn't mention her meeting with Brad Hamilton. She didn't doubt that he'd come back to the clinic that evening to see a patient, but Marian might seize on the incident to link him light-heartedly with the prowler. It would appeal to her sense of humour to suggest that the surgeon had an ulterior motive for being in the grounds at dusk, she suspected. But that was the way that rumours began and became exaggerated out of all proportion and it seemed to Judith that people were rather too ready to believe the worst of a man with an unfortunate past. Give a dog a bad name . . . She held no brief for Brad Hamilton but she didn't mean to be responsible in any way for further gossip about him.

'Did you enjoy yourself?' Marian asked as they mounted the stairs to their first floor apartments. 'I hear that you had lunch with Jamie Sinclair.' She chuckled at Judith's surprised expression. 'Skora's a small place. You can't sneeze on one side of the island without being blessed by someone on the other side! Everyone talks about everyone else and your reputation will be torn to shreds in no time if you give them the least cause. It makes life rather difficult for a girl who likes a good time,' she added dryly. 'But my back's broad and I don't care what people say about me. Jamie's a nice fellow, don't you think?'

'I like him,' Judith said carefully. 'He's been very kind.'

Marian smiled at her. 'You don't have to worry about Jamie. He's genuine. He'll do anything for anybody without a thought for reward and he doesn't rush a girl into bed like some of the men on this island.' She paused, on the point of opening the door of her own flat. 'Any plans for tonight, Judith? I'm going to a party for one of our American friends. Why don't you come with me? They'll make you very welcome.'

Judith demurred and then allowed herself to be persuaded. Used to the full social life at Hartlake, she enjoyed parties and meeting people and she'd heard so much about the Americans who'd come over from the States to work for the Jefferson Corporation on Skora, mostly from Marian, that she was curious to meet a few of them.

She knew that some were married with families and that new housing had sprung up on the outskirts of Skyllyn to accommodate them. But the majority were young and unmarried and lonely for girls back home so it wasn't surprising that someone like the attractive and very sophisticated Marian should be invited to parties like the one that evening, held to celebrate a birthday at a recently opened nightclub in Skyllyn that had found favour with exiles and islanders alike.

The International Club was a noisy and exciting venue, loud with disco music and bright with swirling lights, not in the least what Judith had anticipated. Marian made her way without hesitation to a lively group who'd pushed together a handful of tables and Judith followed with a hint of shyness in her smile as she was introduced. But there was no doubt that she was welcome, she thought, rather amused and slightly overwhelmed, but warming to the well-meaning and light-hearted friendliness of the young men who crowded about her with offers of drink and food and invitations to dance.

She soon lost sight of Marian who seemed to have a particular fish to fry that evening and had gone in search of him. But she was enjoying herself with new friends who told her tall stories and made her laugh and plied her with eager questions and swept her on and off the dance floor with scarcely a pause to catch her breath. It was fun and it was exciting and it was all very innocent. She liked the young Americans with their pleasant manners and eagerness to please and unstinted admiration and friendliness.

Much later, she came off the floor, raising the heavy mass of her fair hair from her neck with both hands, eyes bright and the soft pink in her cheeks matching the warm colour of her close-fitting frock with its skirt of floating panels. Insisting that she needed to rest, she sank into a chair beside a blond man who'd listened and smiled and admired her with his blue eyes all evening but hadn't tried to push himself forward like the others. He didn't drink very much and he didn't seem to be a dancing man. Her head spinning from the lights and the music and the whirl of the dance, breathless and laughing and much prettier than she knew, she smiled at him.

'Hi, honey,' he said gently. 'Let me get you a drink. Something long and cold, I guess . . .'

He'd risen and gone to the bar before she could say yea or nay. Judith looked after him, liking the quiet good looks and rangy build and pleasant manner, the rare sweetness of his smile. The curly blond hair and casual clothes belied his obvious maturity. She guessed that he was somewhere in his middle thirties, rather older than the other men in the party. She was impressed and interested and ready to like him.

He came back with her drink.

'Thank you . . .' She looked up at him with warm friendliness. 'I'm Judith,' she said lightly. 'One never hears names on these occasions, I know.'

He neatly picked up the hint. 'Warren Walowski. I'm the birthday boy,' he drawled, eyes twinkling.

'Oh! It's *your* birthday, is it?' Judith's grey eyes danced with a little merriment. 'I thought it was everyone else's!' His smile deepened. She sipped her drink, and smiled back at him. 'Walowski. Is that Polish?'

He nodded. 'That's right, honey. I'm second-generation American. My grandparents came from Warsaw in the thirties.'

'Where do you come from—what part of America?' she asked with interest.

'Cape Cod, Connecticut. And you're from London,

England. We're both a long way from home.' He rested a hand on her shoulder, so lightly that it was neither threat nor promise. 'Would you like to dance this one with me, Judith? It's more my mood.' The music had slowed in tempo and people were dancing with their arms about each other in the old-fashioned way.

She liked dancing with him. He held her loosely but his lead was confident and he had an easy rhythm. The lights were low and the music was soft and smoochy and the atmosphere was sentimental and Judith didn't mind that he laid his cheek against her hair as they danced. She gave herself up to the pleasure of moving in his arms to the music. She liked the tangy scent of his after-shave and the curling crispness of his hair on the back of his neck. She liked the slow drawl of his voice and the way he smiled and the feel of his arms about her. It wasn't sexy and it wasn't romantic. It was just very pleasant and undemanding and comfortable.

As the music ended, he released her with a hint of reluctance. He reached for her hand as they walked back to the tables. Smiling down at her, he said softly: 'Meeting you was the best birthday present a guy could have, honey. I'd like to see you again—real soon.'

'I think that can be arranged,' Judith said lightly and returned the warm pressure of his hand on her slender fingers. He was so nice. She liked him even more than Jamie, she decided, pleased that Marian had persuaded her to come along to this party. No doubt she'd have met Warren Walowsky eventually, anyway. But it felt so right that they'd met in just these circumstances.

It was getting late and she was on duty the following day. She looked for Marian but there was no sign of her on the dance floor or at the bar. She wondered if her fellow-nurse had forgotten all about her and left the party.

A splash of bright orange in a dimly-lit corner suddenly caught her eye. She recognised it as the colour of Marian's silk trouser suit. As the lights suddenly went up to suit the quickened tempo of another blast of disco music, she discovered that her friend was sitting at a discreetly-placed table with Brad Hamilton.

He was the last person she'd expected to see that evening. But there was no mistaking the dark, handsome head inclined rather too near to Marian's, or the warm sensuality of the surgeon's attractive face as he smiled and spoke with an implied intimacy of manner. His arm was about Marian's shoulders and his fingers were laid against her cheek in an obvious caress.

Watching, Judith saw very feminine and openly sexual invitation in the way that Marian suddenly laughed and tossed her head and leaned against him. Watching, oddly dismayed by a closeness that Marian hadn't mentioned, she saw his hand slide from the girl's cheek to the slender lines of her throat and down to the swelling curve of breast and linger. It was the careless, confident touch of a lover.

Judith turned away abruptly.

'Something wrong, honey?' Warren leaned towards her, concerned.

The gentleness of his tone and the very niceness of the man helped to dispel a faint disquiet about her heart that she had no intention of encouraging. She'd been surprised, that's all, she decided firmly, refusing to feel piqued that the surgeon had ignored her while monopolising Marian. They obviously had something going between them while she and the surgeon weren't even friends, she reminded herself levelly.

So much for his virtual engagement to Susan Craigie—and it had been Marian who'd told her about it! But his relationship with the doctor was obviously a very different matter from his relationship with the dark-haired nurse, she thought dryly, wondering if Susan knew that the man she loved was seeing another woman.

She smiled at Warren, very warm. 'I was looking for Marian,' she said lightly. 'I ought to be leaving but I don't like to go without her and she seems to be enjoying herself too much to come away just yet.'

He glanced across the room at the couple, so promptly that Judith realised that he'd been aware for some time of their preoccupation with each other. She wondered if it was common knowledge that they were or had been lovers. Everyone knew about everyone else on Skora, Marian had declared, untroubled.

'There's no need to worry about Marian. She's a big girl and she knows her way around.' He smiled at her reassuringly. 'I'll take you home, honey . . . no hassle.'

No strings either, she realised thankfully, accepting the offer. He was attentive, slipping her wrap about her shoulders with gentle hands, ensuring that she had her bag, sliding an arm about her waist to steer her through the crowd. They paused by the bar so that he could exchange a few words with his friends who seemed quite happy to continue the party without the guest of honour and teased him about sneaking off with the prettiest girl in the place. Judith smiled and blushed a little and shook her head in response to half a dozen suggestions of a replacement.

She didn't mean to look one more time in the direction of Brad Hamilton but she felt his eyes boring into her slender back as she stood at the bar with Warren and his friends.

Turning her head almost against her will, she looked directly into the glittering eyes and found them so cold and hard and contemptuous that the blood rushed into her face. The way he looked told her that he despised her readiness to encourage the blond American's gentle but unmistakable pursuit. It was just the way he'd looked when she'd met and talked to Jamie on the ferry—and when he'd let her know in no uncertain terms that she needn't try her feminine tricks on him, she thought, smarting all over again at the memory of that humiliation.

He thought she was a flirt . . . and possibly worse. She didn't give a damn what he thought! Very deliberately, she slipped her hand through Warren's arm and, as he glanced down at her, she smiled, sparkling with a defiant kind of delight in his liking and approval and open admiration and walked out of the nightclub on his arm.

CHAPTER SEVEN

JUDITH was assigned to duty on the surgical floor and spent much of the day half-expecting to run into Brad Hamilton. It would be very wrong to assert that he'd driven her into Warren's arms on the previous night. But she might not have been quite so encouraging if he hadn't annoyed her quite so much, she felt. Fortunately, Warren hadn't tried to take advantage of her mood. He was too nice for that, a gentleman in the true sense of the word. He'd brought her back to the annexe and kissed her goodnight with cool, undemanding lips and a smile in his eyes and arranged to take her out to dinner on Saturday evening.

Marian had still been sleeping when she hurried across to begin the day's work. It was her day off and she hadn't come home until the early hours of the morning. Strangely and unusually restless, tossing and turning on her pillows, Judith had heard the sound of a car and seen the spray of headlights across the ceiling. She'd resisted the temptation to throw back the covers and pad to the window to look out. She'd heard Marian's distinctive laugh, the slam of a car door—and she hadn't needed to rush to the window to know that it was Brad Hamilton's sleek Mercedes that slipped away down the drive, tyres crunching on the gravel. She'd have to be very naive not to know what had been going on between the two in the hours since she'd left the International Club on Warren's arm. It was none of her business, of course. She wasn't even interested.

But she still hadn't slept very well. She refused to admit that thoughts of the surgeon had been keeping her awake. She much preferred to believe that the excitement of the evening and the delight of meeting someone as nice as Warren and the pleasing prospect of going out with him again at the weekend had disturbed her rest.

Busy with routine nursing, she didn't have too much time to think about the surgeon until late in the afternoon when he arrived to examine a patient, newly-admitted for surgery on the following day.

Mrs Mcfie was a big woman with a heart condition who was naturally apprehensive about the hysterectomy that had been described as essential to her health. But she seemed to relax as Brad Hamilton sat on the edge of her bed and chatted informally about the impending operation as if it was nothing more complicated than a tooth extraction.

Judith remained to chaperon, hovering in the background like a well-trained nurse, dutiful and discreetly on hand if needed. While he talked to his patient, she listened to the convincing flow of reassurances and observed the famous charm in action. She admitted the enchantment of his smile and the fascination of his good looks and the persuasive velvet of his deep voice, but she still found it impossible to like the man. Particularly as he had given her the merest nod as he walked into Mrs Mcfie's room and then proceeded to ignore her.

Judith might be used to such summary treatment from highly respected and internationally famous surgeons at Hartlake. She wasn't prepared to accept it without protest from a mere nobody of a surgeon in the Hebrides!

Cloaking resentment and indignation with the nurse's traditional air of polite attention, she studied the strongly sensual good looks and the very expressive eyes that could smile with unexpected and heart-stopping warmth or chill with indifference or sear with sudden anger. Having found an opportunity during the day to take a long look at the family portraits that lined the gallery, she recognised the pride of the Hamiltons in the sweep of his brow and the jut of his chin with the distinctive cleft and the stamp of arrogance on the handsome features.

There was no doubt at all that he was a Hamilton, one of the proud and passionate Scots who had looked back at her from the glowing canvas as though she had no place on Skora. Just as *he* did! Arrogant, sensual and quite ruthless, she had felt, studying long-dead Hamiltons. By all accounts and judging by what she already knew of him, Brad was a worthy member of the clan!

Brad rose, smiling, confident. 'I hope I've put your mind at rest, Mrs Mcfie. It's a very simple operation and there'll not be any complications, I promise. You'll feel a new woman within a few days and you can certainly rely on our nurses to take excellent care of you.' He moved to the door with another nod for Judith that she interpreted as a summons for discussion.

She paused to settle the big woman more comfortably against her pillows and to straighten the bed and to pass her a handful of magazines. When she emerged into the corridor, the surgeon was standing by a window, hands thrust into the pockets of his white coat, gaze intent on the swell of the distant hills. He looked so forbidding, so unapproachable, that Judith almost hesitated to go up to him.

He didn't turn when she reached his side. She waited, hands demurely clasped behind her back, knowing that he meant to give her instructions for Mrs Mcfie's pre-medication and preparation for surgery.

Without speaking, she followed his gaze. It had been a golden day, sun high in a clear blue sky. Now it was a splendid sunset, the glowing ball of fire sliding slowly behind the rim of the sparkling sea and bathing the world in a fiery beauty. There was a kind of enchantment in the scene that seemed to hold them both spellbound, linked by mutual appreciation.

As the sun finally disappeared from sight, Brad glanced at the girl by his side, so still, so patient, so pretty as the glow of the setting sun touched her hair and face to warmth.

His hands clenched into sudden fists in his pockets. He'd been surprised to see her with a group of rowdy Americans on the previous night when he'd dropped into the International Club for a quiet drink, forgetting that it was disco night and unaware of the party in progress. She hadn't wasted any time in getting to know every eligible man on Skora, he thought, trying to whip up contempt for the girl.

Sitting quietly at a corner table, he'd observed her prettiness, her vivacity, her capacity for enjoyment and her obvious delight in being the centre of an admiring group. Wanting to despise her, Brad had found himself desiring her with a fierce and compelling flame of passion. He'd been consumed with unexpected jealousy as he watched her laughing and talking and dancing with one man after another.

When Marian joined him, smiling and provocative but slightly unsure of her reception since he'd been the one to end their association, he'd greeted her with a kind of relief. Concentrating on her many attractions, he hadn't been quite so aware of Judith Henty's lovely face and enchanting figure although the girl in the soft rose frock seemed to be constantly in his line of vision as she went back and forth to the dance floor with her various partners.

He'd known that Walowski couldn't keep his eyes off Judith and he'd known the moment the man made his first move, cleverly not too early in the evening. He'd seen that Judith was impressed by the American pilot's charm and maturity and sophistication—and Brad had known instinctively that she would leave with the man at the end of the evening.

When it eventually came about, he'd been taken aback by the coursing of hot and jealous anger through his veins—and he'd laid siege to Marian in a kind of self-defence, reluctant to admit that one woman could be any more important to him than another.

He'd taken her to his cottage, made love to her, driven her back to Skelbeg in the early hours—and despised himself for taking what he didn't want in place of something he seemed to want with an unsettling urgency.

Marian's willing response hadn't eased the need to possess a girl with floating fair hair and sparkling grey eyes and a slender, too-tempting body. Just as Susan's steadfast love for him didn't evoke a fraction of the passion that a fickle and flirtatious newcomer sent surging through him as she stood at his side, trim and pretty in the lilac uniform with the silver badge of a Hartlake nurse pinned to her collar. He was falling headlong in love with his new theatre nurse, he realised abruptly—

and he meant to fight it every inch of the way!

Judith sighed, stirred. 'Magnificent . . .'

'Aye. Very impressive. Nature likes to put on a show now and again to remind us of our insignificance,' he said. He was deliberately brusque. He could charm her into liking him and he knew she would respond as readily to him as she did to every other man if he gave her the slightest encouragement. But he didn't mean to risk it. Girls like Judith Henty were best kept at a very careful distance—or a man like himself might be swept into saying and doing things he would regret for the rest of his life, he thought grimly.

'You must have seen such shows a thousand times, Mr Hamilton. From this very window, perhaps.' It was light, tentative. 'You grew up in this house, I'm told. You and your sister—and lots of Hamiltons before you.' She saw the muscles tighten abruptly in his lean cheek. 'I don't mean to pry,' she said hastily. 'I'm just interested . . .'

In fact, she longed to know all about Brad Hamilton and his family and the lore and legends of Skora, lovely jewel among the fascinating string of islands that made up the Hebrides. She was intrigued by this handsome, difficult man with all his fierce pride and powerful passions. She was torn between an acute dislike of him and a reluctant attraction for him, she admitted with sudden, compelling honesty.

Other men had admired and pursued her, told her that she was pretty, shown that they desired her. Brad Hamilton didn't. He stirred new and exciting and rather frightening emotions while remaining immune to her femininity. She had never met anyone that she viewed as a real threat to her virginity until she came to Skora. But the surgeon had set her tingling at a touch and she was much too aware of his disturbing and potent sexuality. It sparked her to instant response and she found herself wanting him with a passion such as she'd never felt for any other man.

So perhaps it was just as well that he didn't like her any more than she liked him . . .

'Sinclair seems to have told you most of the family history. Get him to tell you the rest.' Brad swung away from her abruptly, heading for the duty room at the end of the corridor.

Judith hurried after him, colour flying in her cheeks. 'I'd rather hear it from you,' she persisted lightly. 'Without embroidery . . .' It was an impulsive rider, stopping the surgeon in his tracks.

He looked at her, dark eyes narrowed and slightly mocking. 'What happened to your trusting nature, Miss Henty? Don't tell me that you're beginning to doubt the man's veracity?'

'No. I think it was the truth as he'd heard it,' she said stoutly, defending Jamie because she liked and trusted him. 'But things get distorted in the telling, very often.'

'Aye. So they do . . .' Brad's tone was sardonic but he was impressed by her shrewdness and her sense of justice. He opened the door of the duty room and stood back for her to enter the small, neat office with its desk and filing cabinets and locked drugs trolley. 'Would you trust me to tell you about myself or my family without slanting the facts to my advantage?' he asked dryly.

'Yes, I think so . . .'

He laughed. 'Then you're a fool—or an excellent judge of character!'

Judith met his dark eyes without flinching despite the

dangerous glitter in their depths. 'I'm not a fool,' she said firmly. 'Obviously Jamie—Dr Sinclair, is just repeating local gossip about you and your family and you must know what everyone says. You're the only person who'd tell it without trying to influence my attitude because you don't care what I think. But as you believe that it's just idle curiosity on my part, you aren't prepared to satisfy it. Fair enough . . .' She shrugged.

Brad studied her thoughtfully, intrigued by her interest and suspecting that it was a clever woman's way of arousing *his* interest. 'What is it that you want to know?'

'More than you'd ever tell me, I suspect,' Judith returned promptly, shrewdly.

'Why?'

She shook her head, unable to explain that she wanted an insight into circumstances and events that had made him the kind of man that she instinctively disliked and distrusted and yet felt physically drawn to despite everything.

'Probably because you aren't the type to talk about yourself to every Tom, Dick or Harriet,' she declared evasively, smiling at him. She wished he would thaw just a little, give her another glimpse of the smile that had dawned in his dark eyes and warmed his attractive face and caused her heart to stumble in sudden, strange delight.

'Mrs Mcfie . . .' he said abruptly. It took considerable strength of mind to resist her unexpected appeal. He wanted to hold her, touch his lips to her soft hair and the curve of her cheek and the smiling mouth with its promise of sweetness.

'Yes, of course.' It must be the easy-going atmosphere

of the Jefferson Clinic that encouraged such a lapse from etiquette between surgeon and nurse, Judith thought wryly, abruptly reminded that this was not the time or the place for personalities. It could never have happened at Hartlake with its rigid conventions . . . and its busy corridors. But she'd never met anyone quite like Brad Hamilton at Hartlake. She was ruefully aware that it was much too easy to forget Mrs Mcfie and everything else when he stood so close, tall and very attractive and much too male for her peace of mind.

'We'll operate first thing tomorrow morning. She's a very nervous patient and I don't want to delay matters. Rod McNulty will check her out thoroughly and he's a good man but we shall need to keep a careful watch during surgery for any sign of cardiac distress.' It was hard to keep his mind on Mrs Mcfie. What kind of fool was he to want this girl with such intensity—and why didn't he just set out to take what she probably offered too readily to other men and quench the fever in his blood? Why was he so sure that he was really in love at last? He ought to whisk her into bed at the first opportunity and then he'd soon be rid of such an absurd and dangerous conviction!

Judith reached for the woman's file. 'She has mitral incompetence, I believe?'

Brad nodded. 'She's had endocarditis for years following rheumatic fever as a girl. I'm looking for an adverse reaction to anaesthesia, possibly on the table . . .' He sat down to write up suitable drugs for his patient and then gave careful instructions regarding pre-operative and post-operative treatment.

Judith listened attentively, making notes, the well-trained nurse in the presence of a senior doctor. 'She's very overweight,' she remarked, looking up from the file. 'Won't you have some difficulty in locating the uterus among those layers of fat?'

'Well, we do know it's there,' he said dryly. 'And badly diseased. I'd have liked her to lose some weight but we can't afford to wait, I'm afraid. She's a very sick woman.' He moved towards the door. 'It's going to be a tricky one, I think. So it helps that you're just as good at your job as Ailsa promised. Between us, she'll do . . .'

Judith welled with pleasure at the tribute to her Hartlake training, even if it was voiced entirely without warmth. He might not be easy to like or generous with his friendship, but it seemed that he could be fair! She smiled at him in swift and spontaneous delight. She'd received compliments on her work from other surgeons. Strangely, none of them had pleased her quite so much as the impersonal approval of the dour and difficult Brad Hamilton.

He went away without a flicker of response to that glowing smile. Feeling snubbed, she went on writing up notes in her neat hand, wondering why he was so cold and distant and unfriendly when they had seemed to be on the verge of friendship only the previous day. Strange, unpredictable man! Hard to understand and impossible to like . . .

But what a surgeon!

Judith filled with admiration as he worked against time, swiftly and skilfully locating and removing the diseased uterus while Rod McNulty kept careful check on Mrs Mcfie's condition and she passed instruments and swabbed without falter at a speed that matched the surgeon's. Much sooner than she would have thought possible in the circumstances, he was inserting the final suture and the relieved anaesthetist was giving a nod of reassurance.

Mrs Mcfie was wheeled off to the recovery room and Judith began to organise the tidying of the theatre and its preparation for the next patient with her quiet and unruffled efficiency.

Rod McNulty fiddled with taps and tubing and checked the complicated array of dials on his machinery. He winked at Judith in friendly fashion, visibly relaxing, the sweat standing out on his brow beneath the bright arc lights.

'Great team-work,' he approved warmly. 'How about a word of praise for the lassie, Brad? She did very well.'

Brad pulled down his mask. 'She did her job,' he said brusquely. 'Like everyone else.' He swung through the doors of the theatre, stripping off his dirty gown.

He'd worked at full stretch without once seeming hurried or anxious. But the tension showed in the sharpness of his tone. The anaesthetist's liking for Judith and her encouragement of it was an irritation that provided an outlet for his built-up tension. The snapped words were prompted by Rod's wink and the smile that Judith had bestowed on the man in ready response. An operating theatre was no place for flirtation, Brad thought impatiently, refusing to recognise an element of jealousy in his dislike of the easy relationship between anaesthetist and nurse.

He was annoyed by the reminder of that serious fault in an otherwise perfect nurse. She was quick and conscientious and highly-trained, slapping an instrument into his hand the instant it was needed, knowing every move he was about to make and exactly what was required of her in assisting. She was cool-headed and capable and utterly reliable and he knew that his own skill was improved by her efficiency. From the first moment of working together, they'd proved to be a well-attuned team and he had a great deal of admiration for the pretty, intelligent girl, he admitted, trying to be impersonal. It was a pity that she was such a flirt.

He'd suffered enough from that kind of silly sentiment when his previous theatre nurse was mooning about the place, fancying herself in love and filling with tears at the slightest provocation. Perhaps it was inevitable that a hangover from those days should increase his impatience with Judith's tendency to be too friendly and too encouraging with every man she met. But he couldn't accuse her of setting her cap at him, he thought dryly. She didn't like him enough for all the allure of her golden smile. The smooth-tongued Sinclair and the impressionable Rod McNulty and the easy-mannered Warren Walowski were her kind of men, after all . . .

Judith followed him into the ante-room, too euphoric to mind the curtness of his words and manner. She could make allowances for the strain of operating in such circumstances, too. '*I* don't want praise but you really deserve it!' she declared impulsively. 'That was very well done! I've never seen a faster or more efficient hysterectomy!'

She had never felt quite so uplifted by her job or quite so essential to the surgeon's task of healing by the knife, either. Before, she'd only been a member of a team, no more important than anyone else. That morning, she'd felt that he was really relying on her and she'd been utterly in tune with his concentration and his determination. She'd willed him to succeed with all her being, praying that Mrs Mcfie wouldn't go into cardiac arrest on the table and doing her utmost to be an invaluable right hand for the surgeon.

Brad was moved by the eager, applauding words, by the warm sincerity of her admiration. For once, he felt that he could acquit her of flirtation. For once, he felt that she admired his ability as a surgeon rather than his physical attributes as a man. But nothing of his thoughts or feelings showed in his carefully-schooled expression as he crumpled his gown and dropped it with his mask into the bin.

He knew too much about women like Judith Henty who would interpret the first signs of liking and approval and response as pleasing proof that he would soon be yet another conquest for her list. Loving her was one thing—and he still wasn't ready to admit that she'd whisked his heart out of his keeping without even trying. Letting her know it was quite another!

'Speed was an essential factor if she wasn't to start fibrillating,' he returned coolly. 'But we're only over the first hurdle, you know. She'll need to be carefully monitored for a few days. I'd like to see her make a complete recovery but I'm afraid that the prognosis isn't too optimistic.' He carefully avoided her shining eyes. The smile in those grey depths was getting to him despite his resolution.

'You really are good,' Judith swept on, risking a sarcastic or crushing rejoinder. 'You ought to be at Hartlake or Guy's or the London, working for a professorship!'

Brad shrugged. 'I'm not so ambitious. I'm more concerned with job satisfaction than kudos. Besides, there's an impersonality about those big hospitals that doesn't suit me. I like to feel that my patients know and trust me and regard me as a friend.' He glanced at the clock on the wall. 'We seem to have a little time in hand before that mastectomy comes up. I think we've earned a coffee break, Nurse.'

The dismissive tone set her effectively at a distance. The smile faded abruptly from her eyes. 'You'll find a pot of coffee percolating in the duty room, Dr Hamilton,' she said briskly, deciding that she'd given him too many opportunities to bury the hatchet so that *she* could regard him as a friend, all in vain. Well, there wouldn't be any more! He was really insufferable!

'Excellent! It seems that I can't fault you on any score,' he drawled, prodding her towards increased dislike of him quite deliberately.

'Well, it isn't for want of trying,' she declared tartly, smarting at his tone and the stubborn insistence on a formality that was out of place in a small clinic where the staff were constantly thrown together and needed to be on good terms to compensate for the difficulties and demands of their jobs.

She just couldn't get through to the arrogant, detestable Brad Hamilton, she thought impatiently, turning away. He wouldn't let her within a mile of his liking or friendship although he might grudgingly admit her worth to him in Theatres. Well, she'd be as efficient as she knew how to be while she was working at the Jefferson Clinic. She owed that much to her Hartlake badge. But he needn't expect her to overlook his infuriating and unnecessarily hostile and even hurtful attitude, now or ever again. She didn't owe *him* anything!

CHAPTER EIGHT

THE DAYS passed quickly and pleasantly for Judith. She soon settled down to the routine of her new job and became familiar with the names and faces of the rest of the staff. She made so many new friends that she scarcely missed the old ones at Hartlake—and she was getting to know the island. Each fresh exploration impressed her with the charm and heart-stealing tranquillity of the lovely Isle of Skora. She hadn't expected to like it so much or to feel so at home but there was a kind of magic about the place that made her wonder if she would want to leave it when the time came. But that was still almost six months away and she meant to enjoy her stay on Skora in the meantime. Despite Brad Hamilton.

She had to work with him on operating days and they ran into each other very often on other days, but she didn't have to like him. Working together in Theatres, he obviously approved and admired her as a nurse but never gave the least sign that he approved and admired her as a woman. While a none-too-pleased Judith went on being much too aware of the powerful and persistent feelings that he stirred in her without even trying.

She tried to dismiss it as mere physical attraction but it still played havoc with her emotions. It took all her time to cope with the unwelcome tide of desire that he evoked too easily except when she was actively engaged in assisting him with surgery. Then, the years of training and the necessary commitment to the task in hand drove every other thought and feeling out of the way. She knew there was nothing she could do about that tingling excitement but hope it would just burn itself out with time. For he just wasn't interested in her at all.

Meeting on the wards or in the grounds, they exchanged impersonal greetings and went their respective ways like near-strangers. Off duty, they ran into each other occasionally but they were only brief encounters.

Most of her free time was divided between Jamie Sinclair and Warren Walowski. There'd never been any man of much importance in Judith's life. Now, there was Jamie and there was Warren and she liked them both so much that she was glad that she didn't have to choose between them for the time being.

Being a busy doctor, Jamie didn't have as much time as he'd like to spend with her. Judith knew that he was fond of her but he was moving only slowly and carefully towards a closer relationship, making few demands on her and giving her plenty of time and every encouragement to care for him. He knew that she was seeing Warren but he didn't seem to mind.

Judith was fascinated by the easy-mannered American. She listened eagerly when he told her about his home in the States, his family, his exciting career with the Marines, then with the police and then as a stuntman for a film company before joining the Jefferson Corporation as a helicopter pilot. He'd been married and divorced and he showed her snaps of his two boys and was generous about his wife's desertion of him for another man. Inevitably, Judith's warm heart went out to him.

She liked his maturity and his experience and his quiet, undemanding affection for her that allowed her to be very relaxed in his company. He was very much a man but he wasn't rushing her into an affair and she didn't feel that she was at risk by seeing so much of him.

Being a virgin, she had a lot to lose and she wanted to be very sure of her feelings before she went to bed with any man. She'd prefer to love him but she felt that she could settle for mutual affection and trust and respect. The kind of loving that she dreamed about might never happen, after all.

But, liking Warren as she did, he didn't stir her sexually. Nor did Jamie, for all the ardour of his love-making. There was something lacking in her response to both men. Judith might have wondered if she was frigid if she hadn't tingled with quite unmistakable excitement at Brad Hamilton's touch and felt the swift and peremptory tug of desire for him too many times. It seemed all wrong that her body could quicken for a man she didn't even like and stayed stubbornly unmoved when she stood in the arms of other men. The sheer perversity of human reaction, she thought wryly. Desire either sparked—or it didn't! She felt that she would rather die than have the indifferent Brad Hamilton suspect that it sparked much too readily for him . . .

Seeing so much of the two men, accepting the occasional invitation from other sources, she saw little of the dark haired Marian. She was either on duty or involved in her own busy social life on Skora.

One evening they met on the way from the clinic after both had spent a busy and demanding day on the wards.

'Just the person I wanted to see!' Marian declared warmly. 'Are you busy this evening?'

'Afraid so. Why?'

'I'm going to a party and was told to bring a friend. I

thought you might like to come with me but I should have known that you wouldn't be free. You never are!' She'd teased Judith before about her two boy-friends, acquired so quickly. 'I'm jealous! Two of the nicest men on Skora and both in your pocket! Which of them is it this evening?'

'Warren,' Judith admitted, smiling. 'Jamie is busy.'

Marian gave a mock sigh. 'I've been working on Warren Walowski for months and you whisk him from under my nose in one evening!'

'You were more interested in someone else at the time if I remember rightly.' It was said so lightly that no one could have known that she still felt a twinge of dismay whenever she thought of her friend in Brad Hamilton's arms that night.

Marian looked puzzled. 'Was I? *You* may remember. *I* don't!'

Judith wasn't surprised by the lapse of memory. There were so many men in the attractive nurse's life and probably no reason why she should recall one amorous incident more than another. 'A certain surgeon who shall be nameless, perhaps?' she teased.

Marian's face cleared. 'Oh, yes! Brad Hamilton. I didn't get very far with him that night if *I* remember rightly,' she said dryly. 'He's much too involved with Susan Craigie these days!'

Judith knew differently, but it was none of her business and she had no right to challenge the words. Marian had never admitted to any kind of association with the surgeon, past or present. She didn't kiss and tell, apparently. She was to be admired for that even if Judith was a little shocked by her new friend's promiscuity. *She* might have two boy-friends but she didn't sleep with either of them! But she often heard the sound of a male voice and stifled laughter through the thin walls of their adjoining apartments in the early hours of the morning and knew that Marian was entertaining another of her boy-friends.

She paused at the head of the drive. She had some letters for the post and there was a pillar-box just outside the main gate. 'But they aren't engaged yet, are they?' She put the question with careful carelessness and waited for the answer with a fast-beating heart. If anyone knew, Marian would, she felt.

Marian glanced at her curiously. 'You'll probably know before I do when it happens,' she returned lightly. 'Trust Jamie Sinclair to be first with the news! Brad might even tell you himself, Judith. You see a great deal of him, after all!'

Judith laughed, shook her head. 'Only in Theatre and he doesn't talk to me about his personal life. We aren't that close!'

'You do get on with him, though?'

'We work very well together,' she agreed, evasive.

'But you still don't like the man,' Marian said shrewdly.

'Perhaps he isn't my type.'

'Thank heaven for that! One lift of your finger and you seem to get any man you want,' Marian teased. 'I wouldn't have been at all surprised if he'd become boy-friend number three!'

'I'm not *his* type,' Judith returned, smiling, believing it. She glanced at her watch and then showed Marian the cluster of letters that Ailsa Macintosh had given her to post. 'I must dash or I shall miss the postman . . .'

Hurrying, she was just in time for the collection. The

postman was a friendly young man and they chatted for a few moments before Judith turned away to make her way to the annexe, taking the short cut through the grounds. It was growing dusk and she hadn't forgotten Marian's warning about the prowler but there hadn't been any reported incidents in recent days and so she didn't feel nervous.

She took little notice of the sound of footsteps on the path behind her as she made her way along the secluded route. It was well used by members of the staff on their way to and from the bus stop outside the gates. She didn't even bother to look back.

She was about half-way between the gates and the annexe and in the densest part of the grounds with the secluding trees and overgrown rhododendrons and trailing bramble thickets when she was seized by an unaccountable panic. It took a moment or two for her to realise that it was the sudden absence of those following footsteps that triggered alarm.

She swung round quickly but there was no one behind her—and there ought to be! Unless someone had for some reason abruptly turned back or darted into the concealing undergrowth. There *had* been someone following her along the path. She hadn't imagined it!

The hair prickled on the back of her neck and her heart began to thump with apprehension. She had no real reason to be afraid, she told herself firmly. She was within shouting distance of help and the prowler had never actually harmed anyone. Or so she'd been assured. It had to be the prowler, she felt. It seemed that he made a habit of lurking in this part of the grounds. He followed unwary nurses on their own or hid among the bushes to startle them by stepping out suddenly in front

of them. Having thoroughly frightened them into
screaming or breaking into a run, he melted into the
cover of the undergrowth, satisfied. Apparently no
one had challenged him or admitted to recognising
him.

Judith looked about her warily. She could hear rust-
ling and the sounds of movement but she couldn't
pin-point the direction. Someone was certainly in the
near vicinity, she knew.

'Is anyone there?' she demanded loudly. 'Where are
you? Who is it?' There was no answer, no appearing
figure. She felt so foolish, addressing apparently empty
bushes, that she was abruptly annoyed. 'Oh, you don't
frighten me with your silly games!' Turning away impatiently, she bumped into Brad Hamilton and almost
jumped out of her skin. He seemed to have appeared out
of thin air—or the bushes. 'You . . . !' she exclaimed,
angry and perturbed.

Brad steadied her with a hand on each arm, frowning.
'Are you all right, Judith?' Hearing her voice with its
undertone of alarm, he'd quickened his steps to reach
her side.

'No thanks to you!' she snapped, breaking free of his
grip on her arms. 'What the devil do you mean by
frightening people out of their wits?'

He raised an eyebrow. 'Sorry if I startled you. I
thought I was making more than enough noise for you to
hear me coming.'

'Of course I heard you! Why did you hide, for
heaven's sake?' she challenged, furious.

'Hide . . . ?' His dark brows drew together.

'In the bushes. It's so stupid!'

'I don't know what you're talking about . . .'

'Yes, you do! You were following me, trying to frighten me!'

He shook his head. 'Someone may have been following you. It certainly wasn't *me*, lassie. You're heading for the annexe, aren't you? Well, I'm coming away from it!' he told her firmly.

Judith refused to believe him. 'You were right behind me—and then you darted into the bushes to make your way round in front of me!' It was open accusation. 'Is that how you get your kicks?' she demanded scathingly. 'Scaring hell out of women!'

There was a sudden blaze of anger in the surgeon's eyes. 'No, it isn't! I get my kicks the old-fashioned way—like most men! Like this!' He seized her small face between strong hands and kissed her savagely, bruising her mouth and shocking all the breath from her slender body.

Gasping, taken aback, Judith thrust him away fiercely and her hand whipped up to slap his face. But it didn't connect for he'd anticipated the reflex reaction and caught her wrist just in time.

'No,' he said decisively.

'How dare you kiss me?' Glowering, she struggled to free herself, so angry that she could scarcely speak but not at all frightened by his strength or his passion.

'I'm aye quick-tempered,' he drawled, firmly resisting the irresistible temptation to kiss her again. She was utterly enchanting with the angry sparkle in her wide grey eyes and the soft flush of fury in her pretty face and he'd been wanting to kiss her for days. He found it a constant struggle to maintain a distance between them— even with her ready assistance. 'And you did ask for it, you know. But you're right. I shouldn't have kissed you.'

Not like that, anyway. It had been too angry, too brutal. No way to endear himself to a woman, he thought wryly. It had merely driven another wedge between them.

He let her go and Judith pointedly rubbed her wrist although his grip hadn't really hurt her. It had only set her tingling in that odd, unwelcome manner. 'By all accounts, that temper has got you into more than enough trouble already,' she said coldly. 'It's time you learned to control it!'

Brad looked down at her thoughtfully. 'Those accounts seem to have poisoned your mind as thoroughly as they were calculated to do,' he told her bluntly. 'Or you wouldn't be so ready to assume that I'm responsible for alarming you—and the others!'

'What else am I to think?' she challenged.

His mouth tightened abruptly. 'I don't give a damn what you think! But there'll be no more such incidents, I promise you!' He had his own suspicion as to the prowler and knowing him to be harmless, he'd taken little notice of the current spate of alarms. But if Judith could suspect him then so might others, he thought grimly. He'd suffered in the past from the 'give a dog a bad name' syndrome!

'I bet there won't,' Judith retorted dryly.

He turned on his heel and left her without another word, striding along the path in very purposeful manner. Judith looked after him, unsure, wondering if she'd gone too far.

She'd hurled the accusation at him on an impulse and she was still inclined to suspect him. But she didn't really want to believe that he was capable of such odd and alarming and disturbing behaviour. She didn't want to remember Jamie's lurid hints about the surgeon's mental instability. She didn't like him but she didn't want to think badly of him. Even if he deserved it . . .

Judith shrivelled when all the talk at breakfast the following morning was of the prowler. He'd been caught in the grounds by Brad Hamilton and one of the security men and freely admitted that he'd been playing pranks on the nurses over the last few weeks. He was a young man in his early twenties who lived with elderly parents in Skelbeg and was well-known to some members of the staff.

'Poor wee laddie,' sympathised Maggie Anderson. 'I had my suspicions from the start when no one came to any harm. Dougal's just a bairn who'll never grow up and I hope they'll not take him to the magistrate for a childish piece of nonsense.'

'Perhaps it was just a game to him, but he gave me a nasty scare, Maggie,' someone objected. 'He's a big fellow and I wouldn't have stood a chance if he'd grabbed me!'

'I thought he was a nutter, to be honest,' another nurse declared bluntly. 'I was shaking in my shoes and he just ran away laughing.'

'Well, he'll not do it again,' Maggie said stoutly. 'He'll get a good scold from his mother and take heed of it, I don't doubt. Mr Hamilton wasn't too gentle with him either, I hear. I expect he gave poor Dougal a fright that he'll not forget in a hurry!'

Marian leaned towards Judith. 'Did you see Brad Hamilton last night? He was here, talking to Maggie. Then he went off with a letter for the post, going through the copse. I thought you might run into him on your way back.'

'I did. Very briefly. I was in a hurry.' It was cool, non-committal.

'You didn't see anything of the naughty Dougal, I suppose? He didn't frighten *you* last night and bring Brad running to the rescue?'

'No.' Judith finished her coffee and rose. 'I'm due in Theatres,' she said briskly. 'We've a full list today. See you later, Marian . . .'

Suitably arrayed in sackcloth and ashes, she was waiting for the surgeon when he walked into Theatres. She had wronged him and she knew she must make amends.

'Good morning.' She smiled at him, warm, slightly unsure. He acknowledged her with the briefest of nods and not even the flicker of a smile and passed her on his way to the changing-room. Judith drew a deep breath. 'Mr Hamilton . . . !'

Checked in mid-stride, he looked back at her, raising an eyebrow. 'Miss Henty?'

She knew she deserved the ice of his tone, the deliberate formality of his manner. 'I owe you an apology,' she said stiffly.

'Aye,' he agreed. 'You certainly do.'

Judith flushed. He didn't make it easy, she thought resentfully. 'I suppose you *knew* it was that young man!'

'I knew it wasn't me,' he returned, sardonic.

'I'm sorry. I suppose I just didn't expect to see you at that hour and jumped to conclusions.' It was slightly grudging.

'Wrong conclusions.'

'Yes, apparently . . .'

'*Apparently!*' he echoed coldly, annoyed. 'Why qualify it?'

Judith bit her lip. His irritation was perfectly justified,

she knew. She wasn't being very gracious. 'I'm making a mess of this,' she said wryly.

'Perhaps you don't apologise too often,' he suggested dryly.

'Look, I *am* sorry,' she said impatiently. 'Do you want me to grovel?'

His lips twitched. 'No, Miss Henty. I'll be content if you take me on trust in future instead of remembering all the bad you've heard about me from an unreliable source!'

He walked away from her, tall and straight-backed and stiff with pride. Judith hadn't noticed the brief glimmer of a twinkle in the dark eyes or she might have felt less firmly put in her place. She looked after the surgeon, chastened but challenged by his scathing swipe at Jamie's integrity.

She was realising that Brad Hamilton had an integrity of his own, however. There was much more to the man than she'd suspected or been inclined to believe. She was beginning to wish that they could be friends rather than sworn enemies. She was even prepared to like him if he would only prove to her that he wasn't as black as Jamie and a few others were inclined to paint him.

She wondered why he was so disliked. He was a proud man, an arrogant man, a stern and unyielding man in many ways. He didn't suffer fools gladly and said so. Yet he could be kind and caring and even thoughtful. He had qualities that Judith was learning to admire and respect, if reluctantly. He'd been badly hurt, too. By too many people. Perhaps his pride was a cultivated shield against further hurt. Perhaps there was a vulnerable, sensitive man behind the mocking and arrogant manner. Penetrate the cool reserve, break down the proud defences and perhaps she would find a man to like—or even to love.

Judith backed away hastily from that last disturbing thought and hurried to don gown and mask and gloves to assist with the first of the day's operations. The patient, a partial gastrectomy, had already been brought up from the ward and waited in an ante-room with an attendant nurse for the injection that would send him into a deep sleep before he went into theatre for surgery.

As usual, everything was ready for the surgeon when, changed into surgical greens and scrubbed-up, he walked into the theatre, where laid-up trolley and positioned arc lights and staff awaited him, the patient already on the table and observed by a vigilant anaesthetist. He took his place among the brightly-lit tableau and flexed skilled hands, waiting for the nod from Rod McNulty.

Too conscious of their recent exchange, Judith fumbled the first instrument for which he held out his hand and it fell to the floor. She met his dark eyes. Expecting irritation or condemnation, she was surprised to discover that they held a slight smile of understanding.

Murmuring an apology, she slapped a fresh scalpel into his waiting hand and watched him make the quick, neat incision while she struggled with a quite inexplicable warmth about her heart. Did it matter so much that he should relent a little in his previously unyielding dislike and antagonism, she wondered, startled and rather dismayed. Not liking where her thoughts were leading, she wrenched them back to the present and the surgeon's requirements and the unconscious patient. A busy operating theatre was not the place for sentiment of any kind, she rebuked herself sharply . . . and she had no intention of waxing sentimental over Brad Hamilton!

It should have been a routine operation. But something went wrong. 'He's failing,' Rod announced suddenly, busy with valves and dials, checking the heart-lung machine and concerned for the rapidly cyanosing patient. 'We're losing him . . .'

Promptly and without panic, the procedure for cardiac arrest swung into action. Rod swiftly ventilated the patient with pure oxygen while Brad began external cardiac massage, hands placed firmly on the sternum and compressing the rib cage with regular, rhythmic pumping. Judith administered an injection with the prepared hypodermic that was kept on the trolley in readiness for such an emergency, and sent a nurse hurrying for the resuscitation apparatus.

Thankfully, the patient's colour began to improve and the initial emergency was over. He was wired up to the electrocardiograph and an intravenous drip was set up and then the operation proceeded to a swift but sure conclusion under the extra-watchful eye of all concerned.

Judith breathed a sigh of relief when the last suture was in place and dressings were applied and the patient could be wheeled off to the intensive care unit. No one liked to lose a patient on the table. Apparently it had never happened to Brad Hamilton, thanks to good fortune or prompt action. She discovered that she had been willing the patient to pull through for the sake of the surgeon's reputation and peace of mind . . .

CHAPTER NINE

THE McNultys were giving a dinner party that evening. Apologising for such short notice, Rod asked if Judith was free and invited her to join the party. She'd accepted readily and with obvious pleasure before he mentioned that Brad Hamilton was another guest—and then it was too late to plead a previous engagement or invent an excuse. Judith told herself sensibly that she mustn't allow the surgeon to mar the evening for her and determined to enjoy herself despite his presence.

'Laura is really looking forward to meeting you at last,' Rod said warmly.

'I want to meet her, too.' Judith had heard so much about the girl who was a community nurse, attached to the health centre in Skyllyn, that she felt she already knew Laura McNulty. Rod always spoke of his wife with such warmth and affection that hc was obviously very happily married. 'Is it a formal affair?' she asked with a hint of anxiety. Like any woman, almost her first thought was for the state of her wardrobe. What to wear—and did she have anything suitable?

Rod smiled reassuringly. He had been married quite long enough to know what was on her mind. 'No, no. It's just a few friends coming for a meal. Very spur-of-the-moment and no special celebration. Laura thought it would be a good opportunity for you to meet and a chance to introduce you to more people.'

'That's very kind . . .' Judith wondered if the McNultys were trying their hand at match-making by inviting both her and Brad Hamilton. Then she dismissed the idea. It seemed to be generally assumed that the surgeon meant to marry Susan Craigie—when two busy people could find time to fix a date! Besides, Rod was well aware of the hostility between herself and Brad and he wasn't likely to risk the success of his wife's dinner party by throwing them together too obviously. Perhaps they only hoped to create the right atmosphere to induce a feeling of friendliness between them.

'Eight for eight-thirty then, lassie. You know the address, don't you . . . ?' Rod went off to change from surgical greens, the day's work done.

Judith was putting instruments into the autoclave in the sterilising-room when Brad walked in. He had already showered and dressed and was on the point of leaving Theatres after the long and demanding day.

'Rod McNulty tells me that we'll be fellow guests at his house this evening,' he said abruptly, without preliminary. 'How are you fixed for transport?'

Judith turned to look at him in surprise. Surely he wasn't offering to take her! 'Oh, no problem,' she returned coolly. 'I understand that there's a garage in Skyllyn that runs a taxi service.' To date, thanks to the combined efforts of Jamie and Warren, she hadn't needed to use it or felt the lack of a car of her own.

'Aye. Ben Anderson, Maggie's brother. But his cars will be much in demand on a Friday evening. I've some paper-work that will keep me here for a couple of hours. If you can be ready by seven, I'll take you along with me.'

It was too brusque for Judith to suppose that he was putting himself out for her benefit. It was merely a

practical, matter-of-fact suggestion that didn't oblige
her to be grateful. It didn't matter to him if she accepted
or refused, she realised. Being a practical and level-
headed girl, she saw no sense in turning down such a
convenient offer. 'Thank you, Mr Hamilton. I'll be
ready.'

He nodded. 'See that you are,' he warned, curt. 'I'll
not wait for you and risk being late for Laura's fine
dinner. She's the best cook on Skora.'

He was gone before Judith had time to bridle at the
peremptory tone and declare that she preferred to be
independent of his services as chauffeur, after all.

She went on with the routine chores that would keep
her in Theatres for some little time after surgeon and
anaesthetist had left, hands busy while her thoughts
scampered haphazardly.

She'd wear the black evening skirt with the gold braid
round the hem. It was almost new and she had just the
blouse to wear with it . . .

His hair had been still damp from the shower, glisten-
ing in the light, tending to curl at the glossy temples and
on the nape of his neck . . .

He'd looked drawn, rather tired. It had been a full day
for the surgeon with Mr Latimer's precarious gastrectomy, two hernias, removal of nasal polyps, a liver
biopsy, a tonsillectomy and a sub-acute appendicectomy
. . . and perhaps he was anxious about Mr Latimer who
wasn't doing too well in Intensive Care. Judith wondered if it was really some necessary paper-work or
concern for his patient that was keeping him at the clinic
until seven o'clock that evening. Whichever it was, it
proved rather convenient from her point of view . . .

It had been a full day for her, too. Until Rod had

mentioned the dinner party and issued that welcome invitation, she'd been looking forward to a hot bath and a lazy evening and an early night. Now, she wasn't at all tired. She felt it would be fun to spend the evening with the McNultys and their friends and she was really interested in meeting Laura and talking to her about her work.

Would she have time to wash her hair? She *couldn't* go out with the lingering scent of ether vying with her favourite perfume—even at the risk of keeping Brad Hamilton waiting while she dried and set her long hair! He wouldn't notice what she wore or how she looked or if she smelled of ether, of course, she thought dryly. He saw her as an efficient robot in green surgical gown and mask and didn't seem to realise that she was a woman, too—and that was just as well, she reminded herself sternly.

Was Susan Craigie invited that evening? What would she think when the surgeon arrived with another woman? Would she be jealous, suspicious—or was she utterly sure of him? Judith remembered the air of intimacy between Brad and Marian at the International Club that night and the conviction that they were or had been lovers. Did Susan know of their association? Did she close her eyes to the occasional indiscretion on his part? Did she accept that when a woman loved someone as attractive as Brad there was always the possibility that he wouldn't resist the temptation in the interest and pursuit of another woman? Did Susan love him—or did she only want to marry him . . . ?

Closing the autoclave, Judith left it to do its work while she returned to check that the theatre was clean and tidy. She refused to skimp the rest of her duties although she wanted as much time as possible to get ready for the evening. By the time that she eventually went off duty, the whole unit was immaculate and gleaming and ready for any emergency that might arise over the weekend.

Making her way back to her apartment in the annexe, Judith wondered why Brad was described as resident surgeon when he wasn't resident at the clinic at all. She knew that he had a small cottage on the Skyllyn road, about three miles away. He always had to be on call, of course—by night or day. No doubt he left a telephone number where he could be reached when he wasn't at home with the administration office. That was an invasion of his privacy to some extent, of course. Somebody always knew his plans for a night out—and a man like Brad wasn't likely to lead a celibate life, she decided dryly. No wonder there was gossip about him. People would talk about such an attractive bachelor without any encouragement, after all. She refused to admit to a pang of dislike at the thought of the various women who must have known his ardent embrace.

She took pains with her clothes and hair and face so that she should look her very best and told herself firmly that none of it was for the surgeon's benefit. She looked at herself in the long mirror with a critical eye and decided that with only five minutes to spare, she would simply have to do.

Her hair shone with cleanliness and much brushing and curled slightly on her shoulders. Twice, she'd put it up and let it down again, torn between hoping to look as mature and as sophisticated as the elegant Dr Susan Craigie and the realisation that she could never successfully be anything but her own ordinary and unglamorous self. Finally, with time running out, she'd left it down to frame her face, soft and silky and gleaming gold against the black chiffon blouse with its flowing sleeves and low-cut neckline.

Did it show rather too much cleavage? In sudden, absurd panic, Judith tugged at the filmy material. Then she pulled herself together and told herself sensibly that the swell of her small breasts revealed by the low cut of her blouse wasn't likely to drive Brad Hamilton mad with desire. He probably wouldn't even look at her twice during the entire evening!

She'd been very tempted to keep him waiting, but she didn't trust him not to drive off and leave her to make her own way to the McNultys if she was late. So, promptly at seven, she went down to meet him at the main door of the building and his Mercedes came into sight just as she emerged into the cool fragrance of the evening.

Brad leaned to open the car door. 'One can always rely on a nurse to be punctual,' he said lightly, not even the flicker of an eyelid betraying the impact of her considerable prettiness on his heart and mind and senses.

Judith slipped into the seat beside him. 'Then there was no need for threats, was there?' she said sweetly.

'I don't remember uttering any,' he returned shamelessly, putting the car into motion.

She didn't see the twinkle in his dark eyes. She wouldn't have believed it if she had! 'Then you have a very convenient memory. Mr Hamilton!' She settled herself comfortably and prepared to do battle. It was safer to fight with him than to allow herself to react like a foolish teenager to his very physical magnetism.

He glanced at her, admiring. 'You look very pretty,' he said, taking the wind out of her sails with the words and the obvious sincerity of his tone. 'Few women can wear black so successfully. But you have the perfect colouring for it.'

'Oh . . . ! Thank you . . . !' Astonished, Judith blushed and floundered at the unexpected compliments—and was furious with herself for doing so.

'Blushing, Miss Henty?' he drawled, amused. 'I didn't think that you were such an old-fashioned girl.' It was slightly mocking.

'I didn't think that you were capable of old-fashioned compliments,' she retorted swiftly. 'I thought you prided yourself on being the rudest man on Skora!'

'Aye, I can be rude,' he agreed, unruffled. 'Cold and proud and ruthless, too. A devil when roused. That's what people say, isn't it? Rumour doesn't lie. But I'm not all bad.' There was a gleam of amusement in his eyes.

She looked at him quickly. 'Tell me the good!' she challenged.

'Modesty prevents me,' he said lightly. 'But you have a lot to learn about me, you know.'

'If I leave Skora knowing only as much as I do now, I won't lose any sleep over it!' she told him tartly.

'You'll not be renewing your contract, I take it?'

'No. Six months of working with you will be more than enough.'

He wasn't surprised by the blunt statement but he didn't care for the shaft of dismay he felt at the thought of losing her—and he wasn't thinking of her worth to him as an experienced and efficient theatre nurse! 'I thought we made a good team. You and I—and Rod McNulty.'

'So we do. I'm enjoying the actual work,' she admitted. 'I just can't stand your attitude.' It hurt . . . but she didn't mean to tell him *that*!

'I did warn you that I'm not the easiest of men. You must accept me as I am for I'm not likely to change to please you—or any woman.'

'Then don't expect to be liked!' Judith flashed hotly, resentment welling at the careless indifference of his tone.

'I'm not too concerned with your liking, lassie,' Brad told her with perfect truth.

Judith stiffened. 'As long as I do my job! You don't have to spell it out again! I got the message days ago— loud and clear!' Chin tilting proudly, the words tumbled out on a surge of indignation. She was much too hurt to notice the slight softening of his voice that turned the Scottish term of address into an endearment. Still not used to his direct manner, she interpreted the words as yet another snub.

She was as prickly as a porcupine, Brad thought wryly. Always on the defensive, disliking and distrusting him, suspicious of his motives whatever he said or did. She was very lovely to him with the cloud of fair hair swirling about the indignant little face and he was much too aware of her femininity in the filmy blouse and long evening skirt. Such a slender waist and such tempting little breasts thrusting at the thin material and drawing his eye with their provocative swell and such purity of pale skin and such an air of fragility that would make any man long to crush her in his arms in mingled passion and protective tenderness . . .

He brought the car to a halt outside a small stone cottage that was set slightly apart from its cluster of neighbours. It had an air of lonely pride, like its owner, Judith thought fancifully.

'This is where you live, isn't it?'

'Aye. You can come in or you can wait in the car while I change into a dinner jacket. But I'll be no more than ten minutes.'

It was scarcely an invitation but Judith was much too curious about him to turn down the opportunity to step inside the cottage that was his home. His surroundings, his possessions, his impact on the place might give her some further insight into the surgeon's personality and character.

He ushered her into a small sitting-room. 'Help yourself to a drink if you wish.' He indicated the trolley with its array of bottles. 'Make yourself at home . . .'

Judith didn't bother with a drink but she looked about her with a great deal of interest as soon as he left her alone.

The cottage was obviously old but it had been cleverly modernised without losing any of its charm and atmosphere. It was a very masculine abode with its soft leather furniture and plain carpets and curtains and the few but good pictures on the walls. He had some expensive stereo equipment and well-stocked bookshelves.

She glanced through the pile of records, mostly classical music. She studied the spines of his books and found a few of her own favourites. She admired an exquisite and unusual wood-carving. She picked up the framed photograph of Susan Craigie that stood on the piano by the window and looked at it intently. The doctor looked back at her with serene confidence in her unassailable place in Brad Hamilton's life and Judith felt a welling of dislike. On a very infantile impulse, she turned the woman's face to the wall when she replaced the photograph.

She lifted the lid of the piano and ran her fingers lightly over the yellowing ivory keys, admiring the tone.

'Do you play?'

She turned quickly. Lost in reverie, visualising him at ease in this very pleasant room, reading or listening to some of the music that she also loved or entertaining friends or just relaxing before the television set, she hadn't heard him descend the stairs.

Her heart seemed to miss a beat and her senses certainly tumbled at sight of him, framed in the doorway and smiling at her with unexpected warmth. She'd known from the beginning that she responded instinctively to his attractions. But she hadn't been prepared for the physical impact of him in the midnight blue dinner jacket and powder blue dress shirt, worn open to reveal the gold chain about his strong neck and the hint of curling dark hair on a muscular chest. He was very masculine, very impressive, and Judith stared at him with instinctive admiration and the dawning of desire.

His words registered rather later than his looks. 'Oh . . . just a little,' she said, stumbling on the words. 'Not very well . . .'

She couldn't seem to take her eyes from the pulse that throbbed so strongly in the hollow of his throat. It was creating a dark excitement in her blood and causing her to tingle in every fibre of her slender body. She was remembering much too vividly the way he had kissed her and the desire that had vied with anger in her response.

'And I thought you did everything so well.' He came

further into the room, the deepening smile in his dark eyes echoing the smile in the words.

It was teasing but too meaningful for Judith's liking. Meeting his eyes, her heart leaped like a wild bird in her breast. He was much too attractive for his own good—or anyone else's! Too conscious of his maleness and afraid of betraying it, she panicked. 'We ought to be on our way. We don't want to be late,' she said hastily, glancing round for her bag.

Brad reached to pick it up from the chair where she'd left it and held it out to her. Judith had to move towards him to take it. She was tense with the need to resist the powerful draw of a magnetism that filled the small room with a kind of promise. His sexuality was so potent that it quickened her to exciting and very alarming flame.

Her fingers closed over the outstretched bag and their hands brushed briefly. The shock rippled swiftly down her spine. With an effort, she smiled at him, heart thudding. 'Thank you . . .' Her lips were dry, her throat closing in panic, her mind scurrying from all the implications of that foolish longing for his kiss, his arms about her.

That shy, uncertain smile was so unlike the swift, confident glow of a smile that usually invited him and every other man to respond to her femininity that Brad abruptly wondered if she *was* the flirt and wanton that he'd supposed. She seemed surprisingly ill at ease, even nervous. She couldn't be unaware of the tension in him or its cause but she wasn't reacting as a woman usually did, delighting in her power over a man's responses.

Looking down at her, his heart moved in him with a mingling of tenderness and passion. He bent his head and kissed her.

He took her lips as though they belonged to him, Judith thought, shocked and shaken but unable to reject the warmth of his mouth on her own. Excitement swirled and quivered the entire length of her body. Melting, suddenly urgent with desire, she wanted to know the eager thrust of his passion sweeping her towards a world of wonder and ecstasy.

Their lips clung and held for a long, tense moment. Then Brad raised his head to smile into her eyes, very sure of her eager response to the throb of desire in his kiss. The shining grey eyes, the tremulous mouth, the yielding in her slender body told its own story. Perhaps she didn't like him. But she wanted him just as much as he wanted her!

Judith was trembling. Her heart was hammering and her senses were swimming and her legs were jelly and there was a darting and very dangerous fire in the secret places of her body. All that for one kiss from a man she didn't even like, she thought, wondering.

'You shouldn't have done that,' she said slowly. It was very lame protest.

'I expect you're right,' he agreed—and kissed her again. This time, his arm went round her and she was drawn into the mould of his body, so close that she could feel the thud of his heart against her soft breast and the heavy throb of his body's need.

Judith knew that she should pull out of that urgent embrace. She certainly ought not to be kissing him back with such delight, lost in the wonder and the excitement of the sensual mouth that claimed her own so confidently. She had never been kissed in just that way by any man. She hadn't known that there could be so much magic, so much fire, so much temptation in a mere kiss.

'Judith . . . oh, Judith . . .'

Murmured against her lips, the hunger in his caressing use of her name weakened her resistance still further. Her arms slid up and about his neck and her fingers thrust a channel through the crisp dark curls that had always tempted her touch.

His clever hands were on her body, moving over her back and shoulders in long, sensuous strokes that ignited her to fiercer flame. Her body arched and her breasts thrust against his hard chest, aching, inviting his touch. His lips moved from her mouth to the long lines of her slender throat in slow, burning caress and she shivered as they reached the swell of her breast and lingered. He was making love to her like an expert, sweeping her beyond all caring and all conscious thought so that she was simply a woman on fire. Nothing seemed to matter but the touch of his seeking mouth and the urgency of his hard body moving against her, taking her into deeper and more dangerous waters on a tidalwave of longing.

Judith clung to him, filled with new and tremulous wanting and discovering how it was possible for a woman to forget everything but the promise of excitement and ecstasy in a man's arms.

He brought up his head to kiss her and his hand curved about her breast in tentative caress. Judith covered his hand with her own, holding it to her. It was question and answer, echoed in the sudden deepening of his kiss and her ready response.

She was on the very brink of surrender . . .

CHAPTER TEN

BRAD straightened, struggling with the fierce desire that threatened to consume them both if he lost control. She went to his head like wine. She was so yielding in his arms, so responsive to his kiss and his touch and the need of his body.

He held her, twining the silken strands of her long hair about his fingers and carrying them to his lips. The scent of her was in his nostrils, mysterious and exciting woman. The teasing thrust of her breasts against him as she leaned up to press her lips to the pulse in the hollow of his throat and press her body close in unmistakable invitation sent passion soaring, near to overwhelming him.

The fierce, relentless flame was like nothing he had ever known for any woman in the past. She was on fire, too. One kiss and she'd melted, taking him by surprise. Why shouldn't he take what she was offering? Why did he hesitate?

Brad knew it was because he didn't want to take her lightly and casually as if she was of little importance in his life. He wanted to build a lasting relationship on the foundation of something more concrete than sexual attraction—and he wanted to build it slowly and surely. If he reached out for the careless rapture of the present he might be forfeiting the chance of winning her love in the future.

So he struggled with the storm of passion that filled his

heart as much as his tormented body. He was ruefully aware that the excitement he evoked in Judith had nothing to do with loving him. Her eager response had convinced him that she was no virgin. She was so ready to melt into his arms that he couldn't doubt her experience or her enjoyment of sexual delight. Well, he had no right to resent the fact or to reproach her, he told himself firmly—even if the mere thought of her in someone else's arms stirred him to a blaze of anger.

Woman-like, Judith was quick to sense his resistance to the danger of that heady lovemaking—and she didn't know whether to feel relieved or rebuffed.

She looked up at him, doubtful. 'Don't you want me?' she asked softly.

His arms tightened about her fiercely. 'You know damn well that I do! Too much!'

Her smile was warmly encouraging, unconsciously provocative. 'And I thought you didn't like me, Mr Hamilton,' she teased. Much to her surprise, she'd discovered that she didn't dislike him, after all. Despite everything, she liked him rather too much and that was more of a danger than the desire he'd triggered into fiercely throbbing life with just one kiss. She couldn't afford to fall in love with Brad Hamilton, she knew. Only heartache and humiliation would follow if she walked along that road. For there was Susan Craigie. There was the impossibility that he would ever love her in return. She was not so foolish as to attach too much importance to the way he kissed and held her, body throbbing with desire. He was a sensual man and she had been all impulsive invitation. It wasn't love on either side, she told herself firmly.

Brad stiffened at the light, confident words. She had a

powerful weapon in her enchanting and exciting femininity—and, like too many women, she didn't hesitate to use it. She was too sure that she'd made another conquest and his pride reared instantly, defensively.

Hadn't he suffered enough through a woman who'd known and exercised her power over men and played one off against the other until the bond of affection between cousins as close as brothers had snapped under the weight of jealousy and suspicion? He'd never forgiven Shona. What kind of fool was he to suppose himself in love with someone too like Shona for comfort or peace of mind?

Abruptly, he put Judith away from him. Suddenly bereft of the support of his strong arm, she staggered slightly. Instinctively, she clutched at him. He moved out of her reach, thrusting his hands through his dark hair. She looked at him, puzzled, slightly dismayed.

'Liking has nothing to do with it,' he said brusquely. 'You don't like *me* but your body doesn't seem to know it. It just responds to a natural instinct. So does mine. It's a matter of chemistry.'

Chilled and feeling cheapened by his tone rather than the curt words, Judith stared at him. 'That's a very cold-blooded attitude,' she said slowly, hurt by the sudden rejection, the swift change of mood in a man who could turn from stranger to would-be lover and back again with bewildering rapidity.

'Quite the reverse,' he drawled, mockery glinting in his smile. 'There's nothing cold-blooded about the way you turn me on. What else can it be but chemistry?'

He saw dismay in her pretty face and doubt in the grey eyes. Like every woman, she wanted to believe that he'd fallen for her feminine charms rather than reacted like any red-blooded male to her sexuality, he thought dryly. There was no way that he was going to give her the satisfaction of knowing it to be true! He resolved on a fierce surge of Hamilton pride that he would have nothing more to do with a flirt and a wanton who reminded him too forcibly of Shona and might break his heart into the bargain.

Judith didn't reply. Carefully, she tidied her blouse and tucked it firmly into the waist-band of her skirt. Then she bent down to retrieve the bag that had fallen unheeded to the floor when he took her into his arms. She couldn't speak for the turmoil of pain and confusion in her breast. She didn't understand. She didn't know why he wanted to hurt her, reject her. She didn't know why he'd held her and kissed her so ardently and then thrust her away, leaving her throbbing and unsatisfied and scorned.

'You're not wanting to call it love, surely?' Brad added for good measure. It was sardonic, a deliberate denial of the conviction he felt that it *was* loving as far as he was concerned.

She looked at him steadily, proud. She felt as though he'd struck her with the brutal frankness of the words. He was right, of course, she admitted fairly. It would be immature and foolish and even dangerous to suppose that love had played any part in the kindling of their bodies to that devouring flame. But he didn't have to make her feel cheap!

'I know exactly what to call it,' she said, bright and cold. 'Only fools or children believe in love. I shouldn't think that you know the meaning of the word.' She swept towards the door, head high.

In the car, she sat without speaking while he drove

through the narrow streets of Skyllyn. She burned at the memory of the way she'd kissed him back and responded to the pressure of his body and been so consumed with desire that she'd have given herself gladly. She was horrified that her weak and foolish body had responded so readily to the meaningless lovemaking of a sensual man who had merely made the most of an opportunity.

After one glance at her stony face, Brad didn't try to talk to her. She was angry, piqued and disappointed. Hell hath no fury like a woman who believed herself scorned, he thought wryly, understanding and sympathising with her feelings. She'd been close to surrender and he'd rejected all that she offered with her warm and generous response. Then, to add insult to injury, he'd declared bluntly that his only interest in her was sexual. Why should she doubt it when he hadn't tried to win her liking or her friendship since she'd arrived on Skora but had kissed her with rising passion as soon as an opportunity arose? She wouldn't believe him if he told her that he loved her. He scarcely believed it himself!

Arriving at the McNulty's house, he turned off the ignition. Judith didn't seem to know that the car had stopped. She was staring straight ahead, lips compressed, looking pale and determined.

Brad was torn. How swiftly the ice would melt if he leaned to kiss her, to admit that he loved her! How much he'd regret it if she took his heart and kicked it about for a while before handing it back with a sweetly regretful smile! Women were the very devil and he knew it! Wasn't that why he'd made up his mind to settle for Susan who didn't inspire him to anything more demanding than affection and would make him an excellent wife? Loving was for fools and for children just as Judith had declared.

And yet . . .

'Judith . . .' He covered the slim hands that were so tightly locked in her lap, betraying tension. She recoiled from his touch and looked at him with ice in the grey eyes. Brad smiled wryly, gave up the foolish and probably futile attempt to make amends. 'We seem to be back to square one.'

'Let's keep it that way!'

He shrugged. 'Suits me . . .' It didn't but he was too proud to admit it.

Judith got out of the car and walked towards the house, fighting tears. Tears that she would die rather than let him see her shed! He'd hurt and humiliated her and she would never forgive him for it! He'd taken her to the threshold of giving without counting the cost or caring for the consequences—and left her standing there like a fool. He had given her even more reason to detest and despise and distrust him and if she had any sense at all she wouldn't allow him within touching distance of her in future. She hated Brad Hamilton!

The surgeon mounted the stone steps in her wake. 'If you glower at me all evening you'll set tongues wagging,' he warned, ringing the bell. 'We must bury the hatchet for a few hours.'

'I'd like to bury it in your head,' she said sweetly and whisked a smile out of nowhere for Rod as he opened the door . . .

Laura McNulty was small and slight with a mass of auburn curls and dancing green eyes and a great deal of charm. It was obvious that she and Brad were great friends. He greeted her with a kiss and she hugged him in warm welcome. She was slightly shy with Judith, perhaps having heard rather too much about her since she'd arrived on Skora. But she made her welcome and helped Judith over those first difficult moments when she was sure that the raging tumult of her emotions must be showing.

To her delight and relief, Warren Walowski was next to arrive for the dinner-party and she was warmed by the pleased surprise in his smile for her and the way that he immediately gravitated to her side.

'I didn't hope to see you here, honey,' he declared warmly, reaching to lay a hand on her shoulder in affectionate, slightly possessive manner that didn't escape Brad Hamilton's notice.

Judith reached up for his hand and drew him down beside her on the sofa, all eager friendliness and glowing delight. 'I didn't know that you knew Rod and Laura!'

'Sure I do. I know just about everybody on Skora.' He leaned to shake hands with the surgeon. 'How are you, Brad—and where's that good-looking girl that you're going to marry?'

'Susan couldn't make it this evening.' His tone carefully drew the line at acceptance of the American as a fellow-guest rather than a friend.

'Now that's a pity,' Warren drawled with obvious sincerity. 'That's one clever lady, in my opinion.'

Listening, Judith smiled politely. But she knew the sickness of dismay in the pit of her stomach. Her emotions were oddly topsy-turvy, veering from dislike to desire and back again whenever she met Brad's dark eyes. She didn't know why it should dismay her to hear Susan Craigie referred to so confidently as his fiancée. She'd known since the first day on Skora that he meant to marry the woman—one day. Somehow, she hadn't minded so much while it was talked of as a remote probability. Warren's easy words made it seem not only a definite arrangement but much too close for comfort.

And that was absurd.

Judith didn't mean to fancy herself in love with any man on the strength of a few meaningless kisses. And it would be the height of folly to fancy herself in love with the arrogant, uncaring surgeon. She had only to remember his scornful dismissal of the idea that he could ever love her, and recall the antagonism that seemed as natural as the chemistry he blamed for the soaring sexual need they'd both known, to realise that loving Brad Hamilton was the last thing to bring her any happiness, now or ever.

She admitted to wanting him, desperately. But that was just physical attraction. It just couldn't be anything else!

Having heard Warren's remark, Laura paused beside Brad's chair. 'A *very* clever lady to have captured my favourite man,' she said lightly, smiling. She bent to put an arm about his shoulders and brush her lips across his cheek. 'Very lucky, too . . .' It was said with affection.

'Not everyone would agree with you,' Brad said, carefully not looking at Judith. As if totally unaware that the shaft was aimed at her, she reached for her Martini from the low table before the sofa. Warren Walowski hastened to hand it to her and she thanked him with her swift, golden smile.

'Don't be modest, darling! Half the women on Skora would gladly change places with Susan—and you know it!' Green eyes dancing, Laura turned away to greet new arrivals.

Judith sipped her Martini. 'When *are* you getting married?' she asked sweetly. It should have sounded like ordinary feminine interest. It rapped out as a challenge, she felt.

He smiled, slightly mocking. 'That's just what Susan has been asking for months. I'm on the point of giving her an answer. People have been waiting on our wedding for years and I'd not wish to disappoint them.'

Judith blinked at the cold, matter-of-fact reply that held nothing of the lover. Briefly she felt sorry for Susan Craigie. Then she rallied. The little she knew of the doctor convinced her that she was probably just as clinical about marriage as he seemed to be.

'I'm convinced you can't be as cold-blooded as you sound,' she declared brightly, hitting below the belt with the deliberate reminder of the hot passion that she'd fired in him.

Brad frowned. 'Then you've a head filled with romantic nonsense, like too many women,' he said brusquely. He rose and crossed the room to Rod who was dispensing drinks with a lavish hand.

Everyone, including Susan, had anticipated their marriage for so long that he'd begun to believe that it could work. He'd known her since childhood. She knew and understood him and claimed to love him and promised to be an excellent wife in a comfortable if predictable marriage. He didn't love her but he didn't expect to love any woman. Until the pretty, independent Judith Henty had walked into his life and into his heart without warning. But, loving her, he knew he couldn't trust her with his happiness or his peace of mind. Loving her, he knew he would probably settle for Susan's cool-headed plans for his future . . .

Judith flushed at the set-down.

'Caught him on the raw,' Warren murmured.

'So it seems . . .'

'You aren't the only one to imply that it isn't a love match,' he said comfortingly.

'I don't know what it is. I just didn't like the way he spoke. He really is the most detestable man!' she said impulsively, still smarting.

'Why, honey! Half the women on Skora are mad about Brad Hamilton,' he drawled, eyes twinkling.

'I think that's a legend put about by Brad Hamilton!' she returned lightly, slightly tart.

She didn't enjoy the evening, though it had all the right ingredients. Charming host and friendly hostess, excellent food and good wine, pleasant people and lively conversation and a very attentive man who made no secret of his affection and interest and delight in her company. *He* wasn't just concerned with getting her into bed as soon as possible, Judith decided. *He* wasn't a threat to her virginity—or her foolish heart. She was safe with Warren.

Brad was the fly in the ointment throughout the entire evening. He was a constant reminder of those mad and magical moments when she'd allowed him to make love to her with an abandon that was shocking to recall.

Having been led to believe that he was generally disliked, she was surprised to observe the genuine affection and respect that the McNultys and their friends displayed towards him. Having been treated to his cool indifference and the rough edge of his tongue too many times, she was astonished to see a very different side to the surgeon that evening.

He was relaxed, willing to please and be pleased,

enjoying the company and the conversation of his friends. He was warm, interested, out-going and Judith saw how readily both men and women responded to that courteous, smiling and very effective charm.

She admitted fairly that much of the success of Laura McNulty's party was due to his presence. Without conscious effort, he kept conversation and laughter flowing and he had the kind of charisma that everyone found attractive and stimulating.

Judith was possibly the only person who didn't come to life at a smile or a word from him and that was a deliberate resistance. She wanted to warm to him, to like him, to feel that she had been wrong about him from the beginning. It might make her feel less guilty about that tide of desire for a man she didn't love at all. But she didn't dare to relax the rigid barrier of dislike and distrust that was keeping her from loving the too-attractive Brad Hamilton. Her body might play the traitor but she was determined that mind and heart should stay loyal to the conviction that he wasn't the man to make her happy.

Besides, he would soon be married to another woman . . .

It was taken for granted by both that Warren would take her home later that night. She'd arrived with Brad but she hadn't really come with him, after all. He'd allowed Warren to monopolise her attention most of the evening, too. Further proof that his interest only stemmed from physical attraction that had got slightly out of hand, she told herself firmly.

Soon after midnight, she began to glance at the clock, one or two people having already left. Brad was drawing Warren to enlarge on some of his experiences as a stuntman in Hollywood and the American was willing to oblige. Everyone was listening, fascinated, when Rod was called to the telephone.

He returned to the room on a wave of laughter as Warren reached the tag-line of his most amusing adventure. Catching Brad's eye, he smiled ruefully.

'You're needed, laddie,' he said quietly. 'That gastrectomy . . . Latimer, is it? He's haemorrhaging and Kenneth thinks you should open him up right away and find the cause. They're getting the theatre ready for us.'

Brad rose instantly. 'I shall need you, Judith,' he said without ceremony. He didn't wait for a reply. He turned to Laura and put an arm about her. 'Sorry to break up your splendid party . . .'

She kissed him, understanding. She was a nurse, after all. Rod was already shrugging into a jacket and hunting for his car keys. Warren reached for his half-finished coffee.

'Two minutes, honey,' he declared, smiling at Judith. 'We'll be right on your tail, Brad . . .'

'I'll take Judith.' His tone didn't allow for argument and there certainly wasn't time for it. 'We don't need a convoy of cars at this time of night.'

Warren swallowed disappointment. 'Sure. I'll stay and help with the clearing-up.'

'I'd be grateful,' Laura said warmly . . .

In the car, driving at speed through the town and out along the coast road to Skelbeg, they discussed possible causes for the patient's sudden relapse and what they might find when they got him into Theatres, carefully impersonal.

Rod's small car drew ahead, rear lights dwindling as he put his foot down on the accelerator. He had to scrub up and check his equipment and prepare the patient before Brad could begin operating. He was the most important member of the theatre team, in fact. The surgeon couldn't begin his work without the anaesthetist's say-so and he was responsible for the patient's welfare throughout the entire length of the operation.

Brad slowed the car slightly on a sharp bend but Judith was thrown towards him, their shoulders brushing. He put a hand out to her, protective. 'Sorry . . .' He smiled, quick and warm. It was spontaneous, unguarded—and her heart turned over. But she realised that she was far from his mind at that moment. Surgeon first and foremost, he was heading for the clinic and his patient with single-minded purpose.

They passed his cottage, dark and lonely at the side of the road. Judith's cheeks burned but he didn't even glance at the building and she doubted if he gave a thought to the turbulent passion that had soared beneath its roof earlier that evening.

The moon was full and low, bathing the island with a mellow beauty and throwing long shadows from the surrounding hills. A lover's moon, thought Judith. A night for love. Her heart trembled and her body quickened at the memory of Brad's arms about her and his lips teaching her new delights and his hard body promising to take her with him to paradise.

She wanted him for a lover. She wanted his arms about her in strong and unexpectedly tender embrace. She wanted his closeness and the need that echoed her own. She wanted to belong to him—so much. She knew that it would be an unforgettable, breath-taking experience. She was dreadfully afraid that it would bind her to him for ever—and that mustn't be allowed to happen!

She tried to concentrate on the routine that she must follow when they arrived at the clinic. Soon, they would both be plunged into the aseptic world of the operating theatre. It was a world of its own, impersonal, detached, sterile—a world where sentiment had no place. Judith suddenly realised that these days it was the only surroundings that allowed her to be comfortable and relaxed in Brad's company. At all other times, the feelings he stirred in her intruded too forcibly.

She didn't want to face the fact but he was becoming much too important. She could cope with physical attraction, overcome it. But loving was a force that swept aside every other consideration. Loving for someone like Judith was for real and for ever.

No wonder she was fighting it with all her might . . .

CHAPTER ELEVEN

THE emergency operation on Mr Latimer was successful in stopping the haemorrhaging but the shock to the man's system was too much and he died the following day. Everyone had done his best for the patient and no blame could be attached to the surgeon or the care he received from the nursing staff. But the unexpected death of a man admitted to the clinic for treatment of a peptic ulcer had a lowering effect on everyone's spirits.

Having the day off, Judith decided to take the bus into Skyllyn and do some necessary shopping. For once, she had no plans to see either Jamie or Warren and could spend the day exactly as she wished.

It was almost a relief to wander about the small town on her own, to eat a solitary lunch and to sit on the harbour wall with the tang of the sea in her nostrils, the sound of almost unintelligible Scots accents in her ears as the fishermen worked on their boats or mended their nets on the quayside, and the spread of sea and sky and Skora to delight her eyes.

She had felt under pressure since her very first day on the island. Too many people were making too many demands on her time and attention and emotions, she realised. Getting used to new surroundings, new people, new ways, she had too little time to think about Hartlake and friends and family. She was caught up in Jamie's eager enthusiasm for her company and Warren's quiet but equally demanding affection—and always unable to escape the turbulent impact of a third man on her startled senses.

Her world had been turned upside down and she'd lost her bearings and she was glad of these few hours to relax, to think and to come to terms with her feelings. Jamie was a dear and she was very fond of him. She was fond of Warren, too. But they were both asking slightly too much of her without seeming to ask anything at all. And she was constantly and too consciously on her guard where Brad Hamilton was concerned.

Judith shied abruptly from thoughts of the surgeon. It was too soon. She couldn't think of him without an unwelcome flood of memory. She didn't want to think of him. It was much, much wiser not to think of him.

She sat on the harbour wall in her blue jeans and thin cheesecloth shirt, slender and pretty with long fair hair flying in the breeze and colour whipped into her cheeks by the salty fresh air. No one took any notice of her. It was the start of the summer season and there were people in plenty on the island, taking over the holiday cottages and filling the hotels and crowding the narrow streets. The ferry came and went regularly between the mainland and the island and Judith sat for a long time that afternoon, watching it load and unload its quota of passengers and goods and feeling like an islander instead of a temporary resident.

The enchantment of Skora had stolen into her heart and it would be a wrench for her to leave when the time came. Judith knew it would be too dangerous for her to stay. There could be no real and lasting happiness for her on this small and very special isle in the Hebrides.

Her heart felt suddenly heavy. The cry of the seagulls as they soared and swooped over the harbour were plaintive, echoing her mood. She didn't know why she felt so low for so little reason. She was happy on Skora. She liked her job. She'd found friends. She never had time to be bored or lonely or homesick . . . not even for Hartlake which had been home for five years.

She decided it was reaction to a long day in Theatres followed by that party at the McNultys and yet another spell in Theatres. It had been three o'clock before she'd climbed into bed, stimulated rather than tired by the night's experiences and quite unable to sleep, head and heart and foolish body still involved with a man who meant to marry someone else. It wasn't the end of the world. But it had felt rather like it at three o'clock in the morning.

Her present mood was just a hangover from those feelings, Judith told herself firmly. She couldn't be in love with Brad Hamilton. She didn't even like the man! Surely she was too mature and too level-headed to confuse love with fascination. Oh, she admitted to being fascinated by his good looks, his magnetism, his sexiness that stirred her so swiftly and so powerfully. But love him? Never! Love had to be built on liking, admiration, respect. It couldn't spring from a mutual antipathy.

He'd never liked her. He'd shown very clearly that he didn't admire or respect her as a woman. He'd told her bluntly that her attraction for him was entirely sexual. He'd cheapened her with the way he'd looked and spoken his disapproval of her friendship with other men—and with the way that he'd made love to her with cool confidence at the first opportunity. Then he'd told her in so many words that he was going to marry Susan Craigie very soon—and she shrivelled with humiliation that he'd obviously felt it necessary to warn her off.

Damn his conceit! Damn the good looks that caused too many women to run after him! Damn him for being the kind of man that no clear-thinking woman ought to love—and did, too easily . . .

'Hallo, Judith . . .'

She turned at the touch on her shoulder that broke into her troubled, confused and rather alarming thoughts.

Laura McNulty smiled at her. 'I thought it was you!' She was trim and attractive in the dark-blue uniform dress, riotous red hair subdued by the neat cap of the district nurse. 'I saw you sitting here when I drove up. I'm on my rounds and had to make a call at the cottage over the road.'

'It's one of my favourite places on Skora,' Judith said, smiling. 'It's so peaceful and yet there's so many interesting things to watch and no one bothers me.'

'Shall I go away?' Laura twinkled.

Judith laughed. 'Of course not! It's nice to see you! We left in such a rush last night that I'm sure I didn't thank you properly for a lovely evening!'

'Yes, you did! I'm glad you enjoyed the party. We loved having you and I hope you'll come again, often. Don't wait for an invitation. Come to see us any time. We aren't very formal people.'

'I'll remember . . .'

'Did things go well last night? I was fast asleep when Rod came home and I left the house before he surfaced this morning.'

'The operation went well. But we lost the patient, I'm afraid. He died this morning.'

'Oh, dear. Brad isn't too pleased about that, I suppose?'

'Probably not. I haven't seen him.' Judith didn't want to talk about the surgeon just at that moment. She rose, glancing at her watch. 'I ought to be getting back. I didn't realise it was so late . . .'

'Back to Jefferson? I've a call to make in Skelbeg. I'll give you a lift if you don't mind a brief detour to a patient *en route*?'

She was friendly and talkative, telling Judith about the patients on her list and their various needs, confiding her views on the members of the group practice for which she worked.

'Jamie Sinclair is inclined to spoil the patients and Susan Craigie is inclined to bully them,' she said lightly. 'Tim Ogilvy manages to strike a happy medium between the two. But he isn't so popular with the patients. They like Jamie because he's friendly and never in a hurry and gives them almost everything they ask. But they go to Susan whenever they can because she's an islander, because she's the daughter of Donald Craigie, Skora's only doctor for years, and because she knows her medicine thoroughly.'

'I've heard that she's a good doctor,' Judith said, non-committal.

'Well, *I* think so.' As district nurse, Laura had plenty of opportunity to witness and weigh up the kind of treatment that the patients on Skora received from the three doctors in the group practice and her opinion was of value. 'The patients trust her and take her advice and wouldn't dream of wasting a moment of her time. She's by far the better doctor, for all Jamie Sinclair's popularity. He's very likeable but between you and me, Judith, he's lazy! He takes symptoms at face value very often and he doesn't always follow through as he should. Susan's saved his bacon a few times,' she added bluntly.

Judith suspected that Laura didn't have much liking for the young doctor whose red hair and light-hearted approach to life were so like her own. She was learning that Jamie's popularity was superficial. Everyone liked him—except those who knew him well and they didn't seem to have a high opinion of him as man or doctor. It was puzzling and rather disappointing when she liked him so much. But perhaps it was merely clannish . . .

'Are you an islander, Laura?' she asked, curious.

'Only by marriage.' Laura briefly took her eyes from the winding coast road to smile. 'Rod was born on Skora but I'm from Inverness. We met when he was at medical school and I was doing my training at the same hospital in Edinburgh. We met through Brad, in fact. I was his girl-friend at the time and he introduced me to Rod. He was our best man three months later!'

'No hard feelings?'

'Between Rod and Brad? Oh, no! I wasn't that important to Brad. He was much too dedicated to medicine. Girls were a relaxation rather than a necessity in his life!'

'Then he hasn't changed,' Judith said dryly.

Laura glanced at her quickly. She'd heard all about the antagonism that had flared between Brad and his new theatre nurse from Rod and she'd been prepared to dislike Judith Henty for it. Having met her, she'd liked her. Having seen her and Brad together, she'd been shrewd enough to recognise an underlying reason for that antagonism, one as old as time itself.

'Oh, you don't want to believe all that's said about him,' she said firmly. 'A great deal of silly gossip flies about Skora where Brad is concerned and much of it is due to jealousy!'

'I expect you're right.' They were driving past the surgeon's cottage as she spoke. Judith instinctively looked towards it in the vain hope of catching a glimpse of him but there was no sign of life about the place. 'You must know him better than almost anyone?' It was light but gently probing.

'I wouldn't say so. I've known him a long time, of course. Almost ten years. He's been a good friend and I love him dearly. But he isn't easy to know and he doesn't give much of himself, even to his friends. It's all on the surface.' She hesitated briefly and then went on carefully: 'Sometimes I think he can't trust any of us not to hurt him. There was that business with some girl and his cousin years ago—oh, he never talks about it but it obviously went deep. I suppose you know about that?'

'Yes, a little.'

Laura nodded. 'You'll not hear more than a little about his past from Brad,' she agreed. 'That incident in particular hit him very hard. He still feels it and I don't think he's allowed himself to care for anyone since—not even Susan Craigie.'

'But he'll marry her!' It was quick and impulsive, more touched by hurt than she knew.

'I don't know. I don't think he will. If his uncle hadn't sold out to Jeffersons . . .' Laura shrugged expressively. 'He probably feels that he hasn't much to offer Susan—and that's important to a proud man like Brad.'

Nearing the gates of Hamilton House, she slowed her small car. Somehow she felt it was even more important to Brad that this English nurse with her fair hair and honest grey eyes and uncompromising attitudes should understand some of the circumstances that made him so proud, so reserved. If she could put in a few good words for him to make Judith Henty think again about the man she was too ready to dislike, then she would have repaid Brad in some small way for the years of caring and concern and good friendship, she felt.

'He really loves this place,' she said quietly, her gesture embracing the lovely old house in its serene setting and the backcloth of rolling acres and majestic hills. 'I can understand why he couldn't bear to leave it completely even if many people wonder why he works at the clinic, in the circumstances. He feels that he belongs here by right and at the same time he's doing the work that means so much to him.'

'Why did his uncle sell everything?' Judith asked curiously.

'All the heart went out of Stuart Hamilton when he lost his son and he'd been a sick man for years. He was advised to live in a warmer climate and decided to sell up. Although he didn't seem to blame Brad for what happened to Fergus, he didn't want him stepping into his shoes—and said so, apparently. The Hamiltons are painfully blunt, as I expect you've found for yourself,' she added with a twinkle in her green eyes. 'Black is black and white is white and never the twain shall meet!'

'He'll still be laird when his uncle dies, won't he?' The car had been immobile for some minutes but Judith still didn't make any move to get out. There was such a lot she wanted to know about Brad—and, as Laura had said, little she would apparently hear from his lips. He didn't talk about himself. Not to her, anyway, she thought wryly. She hadn't encouraged him to do so. She hadn't been very encouraging at all in the ways that really mattered.

'It's an empty title with no land to go with it. A laird without his heritage. Hard for any Scot to swallow—and the Skoran Hamiltons are a very proud clan.'

'He seems to have had a rough deal all his life,' Judith said slowly. 'Losing his parents—and his sister. Oh, but she didn't die, did she?' she amended, remembering. 'It was just a matter of an overdose . . . ?'

'Thanks to Jamie Sinclair.'

Judith's heart stopped at the unexpected words. 'Jamie! What did he have to do with it?'

'Don't you know? Then it must have been Jamie who told you about Catriona,' Laura said, lip curling with scorn. 'They were engaged, getting married. She was madly in love—and he *is* a charmer, you'll admit.'

Judith agreed with the merest shadow of a smile, realising that Laura didn't know that she and Jamie were such good friends. She felt she ought to steer the conversation away from the doctor but she wanted to hear the rest of the story, very naturally.

'He jilted her three weeks before the wedding,' Laura went on with obvious sympathy. 'Said he'd changed his mind. Some of us think he'd discovered that she was only Stuart Hamilton's niece and not his daughter. Catriona had flunked her finals because her head was always full of Jamie. Losing him was the last straw. She swallowed a handful of sleeping pills. Not enough to kill her, fortunately. Brad's always maintained that she hoped Jamie would be filled with remorse, realise that he still loved her and come rushing back to marry her. He didn't, of course.'

Judith's hands clenched in her lap. If it was true—and

Laura could have no reason for inventing it all—then it was no wonder that Brad could scarcely bring himself to be civil to Jamie although work and the social circumstances on Skora inevitably threw them together.

'What happened to Catriona?'

'She was ill for some time. Then she went back to medical school. Now, she's a doctor in a Manchester hospital.'

'Not married?'

'No. She and Brad are very much alike. They both feel things deeply and take a long time to get over them. She won't come back to Skora even for a holiday while Jamie Sinclair is on the island, for instance.'

Judith frowned. 'Why *is* he on the island, in the circumstances? What brought him to Skora, of all places?'

'It is surprising, isn't it?' Laura hesitated. 'I have my own theory about that, actually. Between you and me, I think it was Susan.'

'Susan! Susan Craigie?' She was startled.

Laura nodded. 'I think he fell in love with her and that's why he didn't marry Catriona. I think he heard about the new group practice and leapt at the opportunity to be near to Susan.'

Judith looked doubtful. 'Although she's going to marry Brad?'

'They're taking a very long time to get round to it,' Laura reminded her, dryly. She glanced at her watch. 'I could tell you lots more but I just haven't the time, I'm afraid.' She smiled warmly. 'Rod says that you and Brad aren't very good friends. I think that's a pity. He's one of the finest men I know, Judith—and no one could wish for a better friend, believe me.'

'I'm sure you're right,' Judith agreed, non-committal. She put her hand on the car door, having gathered up handbag and shopping in readiness to get out. 'We got off to a bad start, that's all—and we're both too proud to say sorry. It will work itself out.'

'Without my help,' Laura finished, laughing, looking deliciously guilty. 'I'm not really trying to push you into each other's arms. Warren would never forgive me!'

Judith smiled. 'Thanks for the lift. I'm really grateful.'

'It isn't a very good bus service, is it?' Laura released the hand-brake. 'Lovely to have seen you, Judith. Don't forget to come and see us whenever you feel like it. Bye now . . .'

Judith waved and then turned into the gates to walk along the drive, laden with her shopping. She liked Laura McNulty. She was sweet, well-meaning, very friendly, as open and warm-hearted as her husband— and she'd known Brad for almost ten years. Known him well, even intimately. There had been genuine affection and trust and admiration in her eyes and voice when she spoke of him—and she'd certainly given Judith plenty to think about.

She was still thinking about it as she unpacked her shopping and put it away and made herself some tea and sat down on the wide window-seat to drink it.

Had she misunderstood and misjudged Brad from the beginning, been much too quick to think ill of him, allowed Jamie with his charm and affability and smooth tongue and flattering interest to sway her opinions?

Had Jamie been anxious to deter her from liking and trusting the surgeon and possibly believing his version of the tales she'd been told? Did he hate Brad? Not only because of something that might have happened between them at the time of the wedding that didn't take place—remembering Brad's passionate nature and his quick temper, it was very likely—but also because Susan wanted to marry the man?

Judith recalled the day when Jamie had swept her the length of a restaurant to introduce her to Susan and seized on an invitation to lunch with an alacrity that hinted at delight in breaking up a tête-à-tête. Susan had tried to snub him but, like a man in love, he'd refused to recognise that she wasn't pleased to see him and didn't want his company.

Throughout the meal, Susan's attitude to her partner had been tolerant, slightly indulgent and faintly encouraging. Like a woman who knew that she was loved and delighted in the knowledge and didn't scruple to use it to her advantage, Judith decided shrewdly. Did she often use Jamie as a lever to try to persuade Brad into fixing a definite date for their wedding?

And why was he so reluctant? Why was he still a bachelor when everyone said that they'd been virtually engaged for years? Because pride insisted that he had too little to offer the woman he loved? Or because he just wasn't in love with Susan for all her beauty and elegance and cleverness and obvious desire to be his wife?

Judith found herself hoping that the last was true. She didn't want him to be in love with Susan, planning to marry her, looking forward to sharing the future with the beautiful doctor. Susan was cold and hard and calculating and he deserved better. Such a woman wouldn't make him happy and there hadn't been enough happiness in Brad Hamilton's life, she felt, her warm heart going out to him all impulsively.

As though the thought of him had conjured the reality out of thin air, she suddenly saw Brad. He had emerged from the path that led through the trees to the main gates. Casually dressed in jeans and a thin sweatshirt, he strolled towards the annexe, tall and dark and broodingly handsome.

Judith's heart leaped with the hope that he was coming in search of her and she knew that she didn't care if he wanted her for all the wrong reasons as long as he wanted her! With fast-beating pulses, she watched him from the window and willed him to glance up so that she could send him a smile and a wave in friendly encouragement and warm welcome.

Then she saw that Marian had emerged from the main door below her window and was walking to meet the surgeon, delight and self-assurance in every line of her slender figure. As they met and spoke, Judith turned abruptly away from the window, her foolish heart plummeting with disappointment and a disturbing dismay as it occurred to her that her very attractive neighbour might be the real reason why he couldn't bring himself to marry another woman. She refused to believe that he loved Marian. But it did seem that he couldn't resist the temptation of her attractions even if he was virtually engaged to Susan. Perhaps he knew that he could never be faithful to any woman for long and had too much integrity to risk Susan's happiness as the wife of a womaniser!

Having turned away, convinced that they'd met by arrangement, Judith didn't see that the couple smiled and spoke and went their separate ways almost immediately. When she looked again, dreading yet needing to know if they were walking with their arms about each other, there was no sign of Brad or Marian. It was the easiest thing in the world to assume that they'd gone off together for the evening.

She spent a bleak evening, trying not to dwell on the thought of them together like lovers, possibly spending the hours in his cottage. Neither of them had been dressed for a night on the town, she recalled. She wondered if he'd walked the few miles to meet Marian or left his car out of sight to avoid unwelcome speculation about their relationship.

Judith was jealous.

She admitted it because there was no point in lying to herself or still trying to deceive herself that she wasn't in love with the surgeon. No one must ever know how she felt, least of all Brad, but she couldn't bear the thought of him with his arms about any woman but herself.

The memory of his embrace, his deep and stirring passion, was so vivid that it tormented her with a renewed ache of longing. But it hadn't meant anything, she reminded herself with a heavy heart. He was just an opportunist, sensual and amoral. He didn't trust any woman and so he didn't give himself to any woman except in a casual and uncaring sexual intimacy.

Susan had been a part of his life for years and loving wasn't required of him as long as he agreed to marry her, apparently. He could enjoy an on-off affair with the attractive and light-hearted Marian at no risk to his cautious heart. He'd been ready to make love to her until she'd made the mistake of teasing him about a change of heart, Judith realised suddenly. Then he'd immediately backed away before she could suppose that loving on either side came into their relationship.

He didn't want to love—or be loved.

It was too late for her to guard against loving him. She wished she could believe that her presence on Skora was a real threat to his determination not to fall in love again . . .

CHAPTER TWELVE

SOARING high above Skora, Judith caught her breath in sheer delight at the panorama of the scattered Hebrides, magnificent in their rugged splendour. Many of the islands were uninhabited, small and lonely gems set by nature's hand in a wide and sparkling sea.

Below them were the rolling hills and green fields and the main town of the island that she had learned to love, its coastline gently lapped by the tranquil waters on this perfect day. Looking down, she could pick out the road to Skelbeg and the lovely lines of Hamilton House in its sheltered setting. She could even spot the small house where Brad lived, but her mind skated hastily from the thought of him and those magic moments beneath his roof.

Late on Saturday evening, Marian had brought him back to her apartment. Judith hadn't seen the surgeon but she'd heard a man's deep voice, almost immediately drowned by the sound of music. Heaven knew what time he'd left! Judith had been in bed and vainly trying to close her mind to unwelcome images and go to sleep when she heard the slam of a door announcing his departure. She'd refused to look at the clock and she'd fiercely resisted the impulse to get out of bed and go to the window to watch him leaving the annexe.

She had deliberately avoided an encounter with Marian because she didn't want to hear all about the marvellous evening that her friend had spent with Brad

Hamilton— and Marian did tend to talk too much about her various conquests. She hadn't seen Brad, either— and she was dreading the next day when she would be forced into his company yet again. However, there would be the excitement and interest of a visit from a famous cardiac surgeon to ease her through the day.

Sir Hartley Drummond was coming to Skora to perform a very delicate piece of heart surgery, the insertion of a by-pass valve into a patient with a serious heart condition. She and Warren were on their way to meet him at Fergin Airport and transport him by helicopter to Skora. Judith knew the surgeon from her days at Hartlake. She wasn't expecting to assist, of course. He would be accompanied by an assistant surgeon and an instrument nurse experienced in cardiac surgery.

Warren smiled at her rapt expression. He handled the controls with practised ease, nosing the helicopter in the direction of the mainland. 'Nice, honey?'

'Oh . . . beyond description!' It was fantastic, marvellous, enthralling, breathtaking—but she was too overwhelmed to find any of the words. It was her first helicopter flight, a totally new experience.

'How are the butterflies?'

'Settling down.' Briefly, she touched his arm in a gesture of affection and gratitude for his easy understanding. He'd known she was nervous although she'd put a brave face on it.

She hadn't liked the sudden lift as the helicopter rose into the air and it seemed that she'd left her stomach on the ground. She didn't much like the way that the wind buffeted the craft and seemed to send them off course, or the feeling that it was a flimsy mode of transport for all weathers. But Warren was a very experienced pilot and she didn't really doubt that she was safe in his hands and it was certainly a quick and convenient method of travel. It seemed to Judith scarcely any time at all before they were descending to land at the airport.

They had time to kill before Sir Hartley's plane was due and Warren took her into the Pilot's Club for a drink. Relaxing, Judith smiled at him. He was such a dear. She had become very fond of him and it delighted her that he was obviously known and well liked by the airport staff.

He was a man to like, to trust. Possibly a man to love, too—if she hadn't lost her head and her heart and rushed into loving a very different kind of man. A man who would never love her, she thought ruefully.

She was an awful fool. She'd known from the first day on Skora that Brad Hamilton spelled danger. Why hadn't she realised exactly where the danger lay and kept well away from the disastrous pit of loving him? There was no rhyme or reason to the way she felt about him. There was no future to it, either. And, for all the strides made by modern medicine in recent years, there didn't seem to be any cure for the ailment called love any more than there was for the common cold! Adam and Eve had probably suffered from both in the beautiful but treacherous Garden of Eden.

'Honey, you're looking kinda sad. What's wrong?' Warren reached for her hand and folded it firmly in his own.

The warm sympathy and genuine concern seemed to pierce her heart and suddenly the tears welled, sparkling on her long lashes and betraying that her emotions were much too near the surface. She managed a smile for him but she was too choked for words.

He leaned to put an arm about her, heedless of watching and curious eyes. 'Hey, Jude!' It was very gentle, slightly teasing, full of loving. He knew that she liked the songs made famous by the Beatles. *Honey* was a casual endearment that anyone might hear. But he called her *Jude* in just that way in intimate moments when they were particularly close. 'Whatever it is that's troubling you, we can work it out,' he said softly, smiling into the tear-filled eyes. 'With love from me to you . . .'

'Oh, Warren!' Judith was deeply moved by the quiet and meaningful words and very concerned because he spoke as though he really did love her and she didn't want that complication. She had nothing to give him in return but the affection that he already had in full measure.

He patted her cheek in a caress. 'Just tell what's on your mind.'

She rubbed her cheek against his long, strong fingers in an impulsive and very endearing gesture of affection. 'Oh, nothing . . . really!' she averred, woman-like.

Warren grinned. 'Meaning everything that really matters, I guess,' he said shrewdly. He sobered, looking deep into wide grey eyes that looked back at him so ruefully. 'All you need is love—and he doesn't know you exist.' He smiled wryly.

'Who doesn't?' Judith was instantly on the defensive. 'I don't know what you mean!'

'Hey, Jude!' he said again, reproachfully. 'We don't play games—remember? I'm too old and you're too sensible. We're both talking about Brad. Aren't we?'

She sighed, surrendered. 'Yes, I suppose so.' She gave a rueful laugh. 'I didn't know that I'm so transparent!'

'I knew before you did, honey,' he said with truth. 'There's nothing like loving to clarify the vision.'

'Don't love me, Warren!' She exclaimed, quick and regretful. She was saddened that he should care so much while the man she wanted didn't care at all. Life was like that, she knew. But it was dreadfully dismaying.

He smiled, reassuring. 'Loving you is easy and it's good and you don't have to feel guilty,' he said gently. 'We have a very special relationship and I'm not pressing for more. I'm here if you want me. I'm here if you don't. I just want you to be happy.'

He hadn't pressed for more in all the weeks that they'd known each other and Judith had appreciated and admired his restraint. They did have a very special kind of relationship, close and dependable and heart-warming, and she felt that they would always be friends, come what may.

If only she could have loved him a little, she thought heavily. It might have kept her from loving Brad such a lot! If only there had been one small spark of sexual attraction in her feeling for Warren, she might even have married him if he'd wished it, believing that they could build on a foundation of affection and trust and under-standing. But she knew it would be very wrong to marry a man who didn't stir her to the slightest response, knowing how readily her body could be fired by the merest touch of another man's hand.

Marriage without mutual love might work out very well as long as two people could reach each other through the medium of a satisfying sexual relationship, she felt. But Judith couldn't believe that frigidity in a wife could augur for a successful marriage even if the loving was there in other ways. Real and lasting love needed the vital ingredient that Brad called chemistry, after all.

'I love him,' she said abruptly, and saying it aloud made it suddenly very real and very concrete for the first time. 'And I don't even know *why*,' she added with a touching helplessness. 'I'm not even sure that I like him!'

Warren nodded, understanding. 'Sure you like him. Whether you know it or not,' he said quietly. 'So what are you going to do?'

'What can I do? He just isn't interested.' Judith smiled bravely, facing facts.

'You're a woman, honey,' he drawled, eyes twinkling. 'Make him interested. You know all the ways.'

'I don't think I do . . .'

'Sure you do!'

'Perhaps I can get him interested. But I can't make him love me,' she protested.

He shrugged. 'One thing often leads to another. In my experience, women always get what they want.'

She shook her head, sadly. 'Not in this case.'

'Don't be defeatist, honey.' He leaned to look through the window at an approaching plane. 'Here comes our bird!' He downed the last of his drink, stood up and they walked together out of the Club and across the tarmac towards the Arrivals Lounge. 'If you want something enough you can make it happen,' he said abruptly. 'But there's an old Chinese proverb that I'd like you to bear in mind. It says, "*Be careful what you set your heart on for you'll certainly attain it!*"' Warren smiled at her puzzled expression. 'Think about it, Judith . . .'

The silver-haired Sir Hartley was courteous, very charming. Judith was flattered that the eminent surgeon not only recognised her but appeared to remember her work in Theatres at Hartlake.

'We've never worked together, Miss Henty. But my colleagues at Hartlake have often praised your excellence as a theatre nurse. I hope you will act as my instrument nurse tomorrow? Unfortunately, my usual nurse was taken ill last night and couldn't come with me. As soon as I heard that you were employed by the Jefferson Clinic, I knew that I wouldn't need any other replacement.'

Judith was pleased but doubtful. 'It would be a privilege to assist but I'm not very experienced in cardiac surgery, I'm afraid, Sir Hartley . . .'

He smiled genially. 'Well, I am, my dear. I'll see you safely through and Howard will run over procedure with you beforehand. That's settled!' He turned to Warren to ask how long the helicopter trip took and if flying conditions were quite favourable.

Judith sympathised with his slight uneasiness. She'd felt exactly the same way that morning when Ailsa Macintosh asked her to accompany Warren to Fergin to meet the surgeon.

She shook hands with Jeremy Howard, his assistant. He was small and rotund and brisk and anxious to assure her that he'd put in a good word for her with Sir Hartley. She had some very good friends at Hartlake and she'd earned an excellent reputation for herself as a theatre nurse at the famous hospital. What on earth had brought her to this far-flung neck of the woods when she might have been Theatre Sister at Hartlake in due course?

Judith smiled. 'Too much competition,' she declared lightly. 'Hartlake has so many good nurses that I was just a very small fish in a very big pool. Here, I'm in charge of

Theatres *and* get the opportunity to assist Sir Hartley.
That couldn't have happened at Hartlake!'

She wouldn't have met Brad Hamilton if she'd remained at Hartlake, either. For all the dismay and
despair and potential heartache of the situation, Judith
couldn't regret that she loved him. It was an enriching
experience even if her emotions were too entangled
right now to be detached about it. It brought new
understanding, new insight, new awareness to heart and
mind and body.

Judith was too level-headed to suppose that the rest of
her life would be empty and meaningless and terribly
bleak because she loved a man who didn't love her. It
just felt that way at the moment. In time, she would get
over him and find a kind of happiness with someone else,
she told herself firmly. Even if first love was lasting love,
lingering in heart and mind for ever . . .

Brad was waiting for them with his car when they
arrived at the factory. He looked so handsome in the
formal grey suit, dark hair gleaming in the bright sunshine, a ready smile for the two surgeons, that Judith felt
a tug at her heart.

Having played his part by ferrying the party to the
island from Fergin, Warren melted into the background
and Judith found herself sitting with Sir Hartley in the
back of the Mercedes for the short drive to the clinic. A
suite of rooms had been booked for the two men at the
Skyllyn Hotel and the managing director of the Jefferson
Corporation's Skoran enterprise was entertaining them
to dinner that evening at his home. They would pause
briefly *en route* to Skyllyn to have afternoon tea with
Ailsa Macintosh and the rest of the reception commit-
tee.

In the bustle of exchanged greetings, no one but Judith had noticed that Brad didn't say a word to her. She hadn't seen or spoken to him since he'd operated for the second time on Mr Latimer except for that brief glimpse of him when he'd been on his way to meet Marian. She realised that she'd been hungering for the sight of him, the sound of his voice, the slightest touch of his hand. There was no satisfaction in being virtually ignored. But she acquitted him of deliberate discourtesy. He had been fully occupied in greeting Sir Hartley and his assistant, making polite enquiry about the journey and explaining the hotel and evening arrangements and ushering the small party towards his parked car.

She took comfort from the thought that he took the first opportunity that offered for a private word with her. She was standing by the window in Ailsa's comfortable sitting-room, briefly relieved of the necessity of paying polite attention to Jeremy Howard's monologue as he turned in response to a word from Sir Hartley, when Brad came across the room to her with the cup of tea that Ailsa had poured for her.

'Tea, Judith?'

She took the cup from his hand, careful not to let their fingers brush. 'Thank you.'

'How was your first trip in a helicopter?'

She was grateful for the unexpectedly friendly warmth of his tone and hoped it wasn't entirely for the benefit of listening ears. 'Hairy!'

He smiled. 'Sir Hartley tells me that you're assisting as his instrument nurse tomorrow. How do you feel about that?'

'Do I have a choice?' she demanded dryly. 'He insists that I'm perfectly capable.'

'So you are.' His smiled deepened, became warmer, catching at her heart. 'I'll be there, too. If that helps.'

She nodded. 'It helps.' She didn't dare to meet the dark eyes in case her own betrayed just what it meant to have him near—even in the aseptic and impersonal surroundings of an operating theatre!

'You're not afraid of the great man, surely?' It was almost teasing, gently mocking, not at all unkind.

'I'm not afraid of any man,' she returned lightly.

'Aye, you've plenty of spirit.'

It sounded like reluctant admiration. 'I'm not sure you approve,' she challenged, looking up at him with a swift, golden smile.

Brad looked into the shining eyes set in an enchantingly pretty face and hardened his heart against the unmistakable invitation and provocation in their depths. She knew just what she did to him, he thought grimly. Heaven forbid that she should ever discover how much he loved her! 'My approval can't matter while you've Walowski and Sinclair dancing to your tune,' he said abruptly and moved away.

Judith continued to look out of the window, thankful that no one came to talk to her, glad of a breathing-space so that she could master the swirling flood of emotion.

In any other man, she'd have said that his brusque words had been motivated by jealousy. But he had no reason to be jealous of Jamie or Warren. She could have a dozen men in her life and it wouldn't matter to him.

In any other man, she'd have said that he was keeping her at a careful distance because he couldn't trust himself not to fall in love with her.

But he wasn't any other man. He was Brad, remote and reserved and reticent, passionate and proud and prejudiced, demanding and difficult and much too dear. She didn't know why she loved him. She didn't know why every nerve, every fibre, every beat of her heart was caught up in loving and wanting and need for a man she had never even wanted to like when she first arrived on Skora.

Be careful what you set your heart on . . . well, she'd set her heart on Brad Hamilton and she longed for him to love and want her! She'd set her heart on the impossible but if she should attain it by some miracle she knew that there would never be any regrets for her.

She slipped away, stifled by the formal atmosphere, needing desperately to be alone with her thoughts. She ought to hurry to her apartment in the annexe and get out her books and swot up procedure for tomorrow's operation, she knew. Instead, she went for a walk in the late afternoon sunshine, making her way out of the grounds and across the springy meadow that edged the sea, risking the heels of her flimsy summer sandals.

Then, careless of her lemon silk suit with its fashionably pleated skirt and blouson top, she found a seat on a rock and cupped her chin in her hands and allowed herself to dream to the song of the sea and the cry of the seagulls and the enchantment that was Skora. Absurd, impossible, delightful dreams. The dreams of a girl in love for the very first time and discovering that she was an incurable romantic instead of the level-headed, cautious and thoroughly sensible product of a Hartlake training. She'd been all nurse for five years. Suddenly, she was all woman.

Judith sat for a long time while the sun travelled lower in the sky, absorbing the peace of her surroundings and trying to come to terms with things as they were. She

remembered and relived every encounter, every incident and every word of her dealings with Brad in a vain
attempt to find out just why she loved him so much. She
could only come to the conclusion that loving him felt
right for her, come what may.

Thinking of him, longing for him, it seemed to be part
of her dreams when Judith heard his voice and looked to
see him standing near, his dark head silhouetted against
the fiery ball of setting sun.

She'd just thrilled to the memory of his touch, his kiss,
his eager and throbbing passion once more. This time,
she'd dared to carry those magical moments to their
desired conclusion in fantasy if not in fact. Something of
her quivering, pulsating emotions lingered in her grey
eyes and touched her swift smile with soft and tremulous
shyness.

Brad had seen the slight figure from a distance and
recognised the distinctive colouring of her dress before
he was near enough to make out the delicate contours of
her face. Knowing himself for a fool, he'd quickened his
pace to get to her before she rose and walked away from
her perch on the rocks.

Now, looking into the shining depths of her eyes and
experiencing the heart-stopping impact of that sweet,
spontaneous smile of welcome, the words he'd carefully
prepared died on his lips. With one last stride, he
reached her and caught her by the slender wrists and
pulled her up and into his arms. With a stifled sound that
might have been her name, he crushed the soft mouth
with the hungry hardness of his kiss and enfolded her
slight body in a lover's urgent and demanding embrace.

Judith had neither time nor inclination to think or to
wonder. She was caught up in feeling, wave upon wave

of love and longing and melting desire sweeping over her so that she trembled in his arms, lips clinging to his lips, body arching for closer contact with his lean, hard frame with its promise of ease for the fierce craving in her blood.

They kissed—and kissed again. His body strained for her with greater urgency and abruptly he pushed her away, chest heaving and sweat breaking out on his handsome brow. 'I want you too much!' It was harsh, agonised.

'I know. I want you, too.' Judith put her arms about him, uncaring if she pushed him too far and over the edge of control. She raised a face that was warm and glowing with invitation. 'Kiss me . . .' He resisted, obviously struggling to keep his head above the dark and torrential waters that threatened to engulf them both. Judith brushed her lips across the sensual mouth. 'Kiss me,' she said again, insistent.

This time, his kiss was tender rather than bruising, seeking and exploring as gently as the hands that wandered over her body to sweep her deliciously close to final surrender. She was yielding, warmly encouraging, inexpressibly exciting and the blood surged and throbbed with growing passion that moved nearer to assuaging his body's need with or without her consent.

Judith sank down to the soft, sweet-scented grass, taking him with her in the way that lips and arms refused to release him. He stretched at full length beside her and she nestled close and closer still, knowing all that she invited and wanting him too desperately to care for anything but the intoxication of his kiss and the delight of his skilful caress.

She was rousing him to fever pitch with her eager

response to his kisses and the light, teasing touch of her straying hands and the taut thrust of her small breasts against his chest and the arching of her body with growing need for satisfaction.

He felt her shudder at his touch. 'Oh, lassie, I should stop,' he said softly, wryly, knowing that it was almost too late for caution. He'd never wanted any woman like this. He'd never loved in his life until now . . .

'No—please!' Judith twined her arms about his neck and moulded herself into him so that the thud of his heart echoed her own. She kissed him with a passion that surprised them both, quick and hard and almost savage. His senses reeled at the impact of an ardour that matched the way he felt about her. 'Brad . . . oh, Brad . . .' She said his name on a sobbing sigh, a plea.

Woman tempted—and man fell. As it was in the beginning with Adam and Eve . . .

In the glow of the setting sun, with the sigh of the sea to lull the murmur of virginal hesitation and with no other words but those used by lovers since time began, two bodies merged and became one on a mounting tumult that spent itself on the peaks of ecstasy. It was a natural and joyous and instinctive giving for each other's delight, the glory of sex as it should be between man and woman, enhanced by unspoken but very real loving . . .

CHAPTER THIRTEEN

As THE tide of passion slowly receded, he lay still, lips nuzzling her own but no longer demanding. Judith, deeply moved by the greatest experience of her life, scarcely dared to breathe for fear of breaking the spell of enchantment that bound them. She embraced him tenderly, love welling in her heart. Wisely, she didn't speak it, although the words trembled on her lips.

He wouldn't believe her. He would only think that the impulse was born of that golden and superb and mutually satisfying lovemaking. She marvelled that it had been so wonderful when the loving was all on her side and unknown to him. She didn't believe that it could be any better if he loved as she did! It had surpassed all her wildest dreams.

Very gently, with fleeting kisses to distract her, Brad eased their bodies apart. Her arms strained to keep him and he saw the shadow of regret in her honest eyes. He stroked the tumbled mass of silky blonde hair from her flushed face, wishing he knew what to say to her. He was still shocked by the discovery that she was a virgin after all the hard things he'd thought and said. By the time he'd realised that he was wrong, it had been too late, he thought wryly. He would never have relinquished that tight rein on his control if he'd known.

He drew a deep breath. His heart still pounded and his nerve endings were still at full stretch. He'd never known such an explosion of mingled emotions.

'Nothing like that ever happened to me before,' he said slowly, tautly. 'Nor to you, lassie . . .' He laid his hand along her soft cheek in a tender caress.

Judith's heart quivered at the warmth of an address that was no longer harsh or mocking or scornful but spoken so gently that it broke through all her defences. 'No, never,' she admitted. In sudden yearning, she added: 'Hold me . . . please hold me!'

He drew her close. 'Regrets?'

She shook her head, forced a smile. 'Reaction!'

'Aye,' he said, believing that he understood. He kissed her, lips lingering, warm and reassuring. She shivered the length of her slight body. 'You're cold!' he exclaimed, quick and concerned, reaching for her dis-carded clothes.

Judith dressed hastily, suddenly shy of his gaze and averting her own eyes from the lean and muscular and splendidly male body. With euphoria fading, she was realising how foolhardy it had been for them to make ardent love by the edge of the sea where any casual stroller might have chanced upon them. Like any woman, she thought of another risk they had taken, too—and hastily pushed away the little anxiety that he might have made her pregnant with that passionate and tumultuous lovemaking. She couldn't blame Brad if it was so. She'd known what she was doing and she'd wanted it to happen, she told herself firmly. Loving him, she'd desperately wanted to belong to him just once at least—and she refused to regret.

He walked with her to the gates of Hamilton House and his parked car, his arm about her shoulders in tenderly protective embrace. Judith thought how won-derful it would be if only he loved her, too. But such a miracle could only happen between the pages of a romantic novel, she thought wryly. In real life, there were too many one-sided lovings and few happy endings for girls who gave their hearts too readily . . .

Reaching his car, they paused and smiled at each other, reluctant to part but knowing they would meet again that evening. Both were invited to the dinner party at which Sir Hartley was the guest of honour. Judith's invitation had been last-minute, due to the non-arrival of the nurse he had been expected to bring with him. She wasn't offended and she looked forward to the evening with very different feelings to earlier. For whatever happened, she was sure that she and Brad couldn't go back to being at loggerheads. They'd shared too much emotion during that brief and unforgettable idyll.

'I'm all confused about you, Miss Henty,' Brad drawled, dark eyes twinkling. 'I thought I knew the kind of woman you are. Now I find that I know very little about you.'

'Perhaps we could make a new beginning, Mr Hamilton?' she suggested lightly, rather shyly.

'Aye, I think that's best,' he agreed. 'We went so quickly from enemies to lovers that we forgot to be friends on the way. I'd very much like to have you for a friend, Judith.' It was warm and quiet, obviously meant.

Judith impulsively turned into him, hugged him. 'I never wanted to be on bad terms with you. You forced it on me!'

'That's true enough,' he admitted. 'I wanted you when I first saw you but you took a fancy to Sinclair. Maybe I'm too proud but I'll not enter into competition with him or any other man. You were aye quick to believe every word he uttered, too.' He shrugged.

'Laura McNulty told me about your sister. The truth, I mean. I didn't hear the full story from Jamie,' she said frankly.

'I doubt that you'd hear the full story from him on anything.' It was cold, brusque.

'Nor you, apparently. You wouldn't tell me anything,' she reminded him wryly.

'I told you that I killed my cousin.'

Judith caught at him and swung him round to face her. 'Tell me properly, Brad! I need to know!'

'Fearing that you've lain in the arms of a murderer, Judith?' His tone was sardonic.

She flushed. 'No!' She hated herself for doubting him but the thought had flashed across her mind that if she was pregnant by him, the mark of Cain might be on the child. How could she know?

Brad was silent, thoughtful, studying the small face with its defiant expression. He'd never forgiven himself for failing to save Fergus on that dreadful day, twelve years before. He knew what too many people said and believed and he knew that few had believed his version of the fatal accident at the time.

Wasn't he the one with the temper that flared too swiftly? Didn't he have the reputation for going in with fists flying or driving headlong at his fellows with little regard for consequences? Was it likely that anyone who'd known the gentle, placid and kindly Fergus would believe that his cousin had launched himself across the boat in sudden murderous fury and lashed out so strongly with an oar that Brad had been stunned and dazed. The shock of ice-cold water had brought him round to find the boat overturned and his cousin struggling to right it.

Dizzy and sick and bleeding, he'd gone to help and been cursed and kicked in face and chest for his pains. Strong currents had swept him away from the boat, half-conscious. Perhaps he should have drowned and been spared a lot of black despair in the ensuing years. But he possessed a strong instinct for self-preservation and he'd managed to get back to the boat. There'd been no sign of Fergus and he'd never known if his cousin, a poor swimmer, had suffered an attack of cramp in the cold water or deliberately let go his hold on life. However it had been, Fergus had died and he'd lived and learned to wear the shield of pride that had kept him from loving all these years. But the feeling that Judith had inspired was stronger than pride and deeper than his love for home or heritage or anything else and wiped the slate clean of all the distrust and contempt and resentment he'd felt for her sex for too many years.

He bent towards her and parted the dark hair at the temple. 'Another inch to the right and we would both have died in that accident,' he said quietly.

Judith caught her breath and touched the white scar with trembling fingers. She knew by some instinct all that he had left unsaid. 'He tried to kill you!'

'I took the woman he loved. I didn't know he felt so deeply about Shona or wanted to marry her. I thought she was just another girl among the many in his life. In his shoes, I'd have done exactly the same thing, no doubt.' He smiled grimly. 'Hamiltons don't take kindly to losing when their hearts are set on something.'

She reached for his hand, held tight, 'I'm sorry I doubted you, Brad.'

The tension slowly ebbed from his tall frame. 'You'd

no reason to trust me,' he said gently. 'We were strangers.'

'I'm afraid I've been horrid to you—many times!' She
was repentant, remembering how ready she'd been to
dislike and distrust him and how she'd fought against
loving him when every instinct had told her that he was
the only man she would ever want.

He kissed her. 'You were very sweet to a dour Scot
with a grudge against women—many times,' he
amended firmly. 'You're a grand lassie, as Ailsa tells me
almost every day. It's no wonder that everyone on Skora
has taken you to their hearts.' He swung himself behind
the wheel and turned on the ignition, smiling at her with
warmth.

Except you, Judith thought ruefully, waving as the car
sped away. *Except you, Brad Hamilton . . .*

She went with Ailsa Macintosh to the dinner party
that evening, as arranged. She wore a short frock of soft
green taffeta and wound her pale hair about her head in
a smooth, shining band. Giving herself a last glance in
the mirror before leaving, she wondered why she didn't
look any different. Surely a girl who had crossed the last
important threshold into full womanhood *ought* to look
different. Newly aware, fulfilled, even faintly trium-
phant? She was paler than usual, perhaps. Her eyes were
bright and her mouth slightly tremulous at the thought of
Brad and how he would behave towards her when they
met. Was she already dismissed as just another easy
conquest, after all? Or was he remembering with a
warmth about his heart, as she was? Did she, *could* she
mean anything at all to him? She certainly didn't show
any sign of having lain in his arms and been transported
to that new and wonderful world, she decided. Perhaps

she should be grateful in view of Ailsa's keen eyes and shrewd perception!

They arrived at the Frankels' house in the wake of a car whose sleek lines caused Judith's heart to beat a little faster. She prepared to meet its owner with a casual friendliness that wouldn't betray her feelings to the world—or to him!

She wasn't prepared for the sight of Susan Craigie, stepping from the car and smiling at Brad and sliding her hand through his arm with a cool and easy confidence that smote Judith to the heart. Quite forgetting that the evening's arrangements had been made in advance, hurt and humiliation overwhelmed her at the thought that he'd rushed to be with another woman after all that they'd been to each other earlier.

Ailsa called a cheery greeting and the couple turned, paused. Over Susan's lovely auburn head, the tall and disturbingly attractive surgeon met Judith's anxious eyes and sent her a very special smile. Her skittering heart steadied, grew calm. After all, she had no need to be anxious about his relationship with the doctor, she realised thankfully. If the lovely and clever Susan Craigie could have touched and warmed his proud heart, it would have happened long ago!

'Good evening, Ailsa! How are you? And Miss Henty, isn't it? I expect you're settled in and quite used to us all by now.'

The doctor's tone and manner was faintly condescending but at least she remembered her, Judith thought, rather surprised. She nodded, smiled, shook hands and murmured a polite reply, wondering if Susan knew how often she had been in Jamie's company during her weeks on Skora—and if she minded. There was a very possessive streak in the woman's nature, she suspected, explaining why she clung so firmly to Brad despite his obvious reluctance to marry her.

'I'm hoping to persuade Judith to stay for a very long time,' Brad said, smiling down at her. 'I don't know what I'd do without her now.' There was a great deal of warmth in the way he looked and spoke, causing Susan to glance at him quickly, her eyes hardening.

Judith blushed so deeply that it was obvious that the words held a very real meaning for her. She saw Susan's expression and the quick, knowing smile that lightened Ailsa's homely face. She was much more concerned with the way that Brad looked at her. Like a man in love who didn't care who knew it, she thought with a startled, incredulous flutter of her heart.

'It's very important to have a really good theatre nurse,' Ailsa agreed lightly to ease a very tense moment. One would need to be blind or a fool not to recognise what had leaped to life between the surgeon and the fair-haired girl with her golden smile and sweet nature, she thought shrewdly. But it was impossible not to feel just a little sorry for the over-confident Susan Craigie who had taken him too much for granted through the years. 'I think we should go in, don't you?' she suggested, ushering them towards the house with smiling briskness. 'Isn't this Sir Hartley and Mr Howard arriving . . . ?'

Inside the big house, greetings over, Judith found Brad briefly at her side, reaching to press her fingers in a quick gesture of reassurance. 'All right?'

She looked up at him, heart trembling. 'Yes . . . I'm fine.'

He smiled, very warm. 'I like that way of doing your hair. It suits you.'

'Thank you.'

'If you continue to look at me like that I shall kiss you in front of all these people,' he said softly, eyes twinkling.

'Dr Craigie is looking for you,' she said hastily, knowing that the warm colour was rushing into her face once more.

'Aye, I must do my duty,' he said wryly. 'And here's Howard making a bee-line for you. Try not to be unfaithful to me, won't you?'

Judith gave a sudden gurgle of laughter as she met the dancing devilment in his dark eyes—and turned to see the determined, roly-poly surgeon heading for her with unmistakable purpose.

'Don't think I'm not tempted,' she murmured mischievously.

With a brief pressure of his hand on her shoulder, he turned away with a nod for Jeremy Howard and Judith was left to fend off the man's earnest and admiring attentions.

At dinner, she found herself seated between him and Jamie Sinclair. She had mixed feelings about Jamie at the moment. She didn't care to remember the things he'd said and hinted about Brad. At the same time, he had been a good friend to her since she came to Skora and she'd become fond of him. If there was any truth in Laura McNulty's theory about his feeling for Susan Craigie then perhaps she should feel sorry for him. But it was hard to believe that anyone so light-hearted as the red-headed young doctor could care deeply for anyone, she thought dryly, watching him start up a flirtation with the pretty Patti Frankel on his other side. She left him free to indulge his favourite occupation, allowing Jeremy Howard to monopolise her attention.

He paid her several heavy-handed compliments in between reminiscing about his own days at Hartlake—before her time, of course!—and telling her that he planned to put up his plate in Harley Street very soon and needed a suitable nurse to be his right hand. The implications were obvious but Judith suspected that he was just shooting a line because he fancied her. She wasn't tempted by the little man's personality or his prospects.

A boring evening was alleviated only by Brad's presence but Judith had no opportunity to talk to him. She couldn't shake off Jeremy Howard for her part and Jamie hovered persistently, too. And Susan made sure that Brad didn't gravitate to her side by whisking him away whenever she could prise him from Sir Hartley. The two surgeons had taken a liking to each other, had much in common and a great deal to talk about, apparently.

The hardest part of the evening for Judith was saying goodnight to Brad and wondering if he would be tempted to linger when he took Susan home. She was a very beautiful woman and she didn't suppose for one moment that their relationship had been platonic in the past. Brad was a very sensual and passionate man, after all. Would he resist an invitation if it was offered?

He seemed to know what was in her mind. He took her hand into his own and there was understanding and reassurance in his slow, enchanting smile. 'An early night for all concerned in tomorrow's drama, don't you think, Judith? We shall all need to be at our best.

Goodnight—and sweet dreams.' He bent his dark head and kissed her on the cheek. Susan stiffened, a chilly smile pinned to her lips. Ailsa looked her surprise. A murmur rippled round the room and somebody chuckled.

Tingling all over and torn between elation and embarrassment, Judith braved a barrage of eyes and knowing smiles to cross the room to say goodnight to the Frankels. *En route*, she passed Jamie and paused. He shook his head at her in rueful reproach, implying that he thought her a fool, and her chin went up and her eyes sparkled with sudden militancy. Jamie and the rest of the world could think what it liked! She loved Brad and she trusted him and if he wanted her she would be the happiest girl on earth!

Tactfully, Ailsa talked of other things during the drive to the clinic. But, as Judith opened the car door to get out, she couldn't resist saying with a merry twinkle in her eye: 'Goodnight, my dear . . . and sweet dreams!'

It was a long time before Judith slept. Mind and heart were too full of Brad and the way he'd looked and spoken and kissed her in front of everyone. She was afraid to believe all that his sudden change of attitude implied. Perhaps she should take care not to build up all her hopes and dream too many dreams on the foundation of a charm that had swept her into his arms on a wave of careless rapture. Perhaps he had nothing more than a brief and tempestuous affair in mind. Perhaps she was a fool to have given herself so gladly and to believe that he was all her happiness for the rest of her life. Perhaps she should simply follow where her heart had led and love him without question . . .

The following morning, Sir Hartley looked and

beamed his approval of the gleaming, up-to-date theatre
in all its pristine readiness. 'Excellent!' he said warmly,
his tone betraying that he hadn't expected such hygienic
efficiency from a small private clinic in the Hebrides
even if Theatres was the responsibility of a highly-
trained Hartlake nurse. 'Quite admirable!' He turned to
the two surgeons who had followed in his wake. 'Shall
we scrub up, gentlemen . . . ?'

Brad was a fine surgeon. But here was a master of his
craft performing the most delicate and intricate surgery
on a pulsating heart, Judith marvelled. Open heart
surgery had begun to be regarded as almost routine
procedure but it still required the skill and sensitivity of a
great surgeon and highly efficient team-work.

At first, she was nervous, apprehensive. But she was a
born theatre nurse and soon she forgot to think of
anything but the patient on the table and the surgeon's
requirements. He was methodical and very painstaking,
patient and courteous, explaining every step of the
operation and telling Judith in advance which instrument he would need and what he was going to do and
when she should swab. Jeremy Howard assisted, tying
ligatures and clamping arteries and separating the muscles of the heart and Judith forgot that he was a fussy and
absurd little man and only recognised that he was
another surgeon who commanded her respect and
admiration.

Brad held a watching brief most of the time, only
called upon when another pair of hands was needed. As
usual, Rod McNulty was the most essential member of
the team throughout the lengthy and often tedious and
always dangerous operation.

At last, it was over.

Sir Hartley pulled off his mask and gown and nodded his approval of Judith's work as the patient was wheeled out of the theatre. 'Well done, Miss Henty!'

She smiled rather shakily. Throughout all those hours, she had been under considerable and unfamiliar pressure. Now, she was very tired and foolishly near to tears. But she set about her routine chores and organised the stringent cleaning and sterilising of the theatre while Sir Hartley and his colleague went off to a delayed lunch before beginning their long journey back to London.

At last, Judith was free to relax. Going into the sitting-room, she found Brad waiting for her with fresh, steaming coffee. 'Well done, Miss Henty!' he echoed.

She sighed and sank into a chair. 'I wouldn't want to go through it again! It was an ordeal!'

'You survived.'

She looked at him. 'Only because every time I came near to panicking I caught your eye and you nodded to let me know I was doing all right!'

Her frankness was endearing. His heart reached out to her with the longing to have and to hold the enchanting Judith till the end of time.

'Howard is very impressed by your work. I gather that he's planning to steal you away from me,' he said lightly.

Judith stirred her coffee. 'He was saying something about it last night.'

'Interested?'

She hesitated. 'I'm committed until the end of October,' she reminded him carefully. 'I'm not sure what happens then . . . what the future holds.'

He took the cup of cooling coffee from her unresisting

hand and set it down on the table. Then he crouched on his haunches before her chair and took both her hands into his own. His dark eyes were on a level with her grey ones, narrowed and intent.

'I'll not want to lose you, Judith.'

Her heart bounded. 'Speaking as a surgeon . . . ?' she challenged, smiling at him.

'Speaking as a man!' He carried her hands to his lips and pressed a kiss into the palms, one after the other. 'We belong together, you and I.'

She searched his eyes, her heart beating high and hard in her throat, wanting to believe but not daring to believe. 'Is that chemistry?' she teased, taking refuge in levity.

'A little chemistry, maybe. An awful lot of loving, lassie. I've waited so long for you and I need you so much. Do you think you could ever love a proud and hot-tempered Scot?' He straightened and drew her up with him, unsure for the first time in his life.

'It shouldn't be so difficult if you can love a Sassenach . . . oh!' The breath was forced out of her by the urgency of his embrace, the strength of his arms. She surfaced from the deep waters of his kiss, trembling, all desire for light-hearted teasing vanquished by the intensity of loving that she found in the way that he held her and murmured her name as though it was a talisman for the future. 'I do love you,' she said, quick and warm and honest. 'I'll always love you . . .'

He drew her to him and touched his lips to the soft hair that had been hidden by her cap all morning. Judith nestled close, content, knowing that she'd found safe harbour for her heart on the lovely and enchanted Isle of Skora.

She'd come to Skora in search of adventure and she'd found love. The greatest adventure of all.

It could never have happened at Hartlake . . .

Doctor Nurse Romances

Amongst the intense emotional pressures of modern medical life, doctors and nurses often find romance. This is the other Doctor Nurse title available this month.

THE CRY OF THE SWAN
by Sarah Franklin

Nicola Page is keen to get the job as Staff Nurse at the Meadowlands Rehabilitation Centre – until she finds that Simon Grey, who belongs firmly in her past, is on the board of interviewers. The four years since she last saw him is a long time so surely she should have got over her crush on an older, married man by now? Why then is she so afraid that if she accepts the job she will be once more running headlong into heartache?

Mills & Boon
the rose of romance